Wild Orphan

Wild Orphan

KATHRYN ADAMS DOTY

Edinborough Press

Edinborough Press
1-888-251-6336
www. edinborough. com
books@edinborough. com

LIBRARY OF CONGRESS CATALOGING-IN-PUBLICATION DATA
Doty, Kathryn Adams, 1920-
Wild orphan / Kathryn Adams Doty.— 1st ed.
p. cm.
ISBN-13: 978-1-889020-20-4 (pbk. : alk. paper)
ISBN-10: 1-889020-20-6 (pbk. : alk. paper)

The text is composed in Adobe Warnock and printed on acid free paper.

Cover illustration by Moon Young Hohn

CONTENTS

Wild Orphan

CHAPTER I

"I'M NOT an orphan! I'm really not an orphan!" The words were a shout in my head. But aloud I said nothing at all. I just clung to my mother's hand as we started up the cement steps of the dark building in front of us. Her fingers were thin and cold.

I looked up at the tall double door at the top of the steps. Above the door was a pane of glass with big black lettering:

CENTRAL ORPHAN'S ASYLUM—FOUNDED 1877

I shivered. I had promised myself that I would be brave for Mutti's sake, but I forgot that now. My foot bumped against the bottom step as I pulled at my mother, trying to hold her back.

"Please, Mutti, please," I heard myself pleading, sounding more like a little kid than an eleven-year-old, supposed to be old for my age. But I couldn't stop myself. "How can you leave me in a place like this, Mutti? I won't know anybody. I won't know what to do. I can't stand it. I can't."

Mutti stopped and was very still. I didn't look up at her for fear of seeing tears in her eyes, which always made me miserable, but I could feel her sadness right through my fingers.

The day she first told me she was taking me to live in an orphanage, she'd come home all worn out and as pale as a fading flower. For weeks and weeks she'd been looking for a job, but had found nothing. That day, she sat me down on our worn sofa, and with tears filling her soft grey eyes told me, "Lizbeth, I've found a job. It's in a macaroni factory, folding boxes. It's not much, but it's steady. It's a night job, Lizbeth."

She coughed a little into her handkerchief and then went on. "I'll be gone at night, you see—and—and sleeping part of the day. You understand?"

I understood she wanted to have a steady job. She'd been working for years—ever since we came to America from Germany, seven long years ago. She'd stretched her savings to "keep body and soul together" as she put it. Then, when her savings ran out, she started sewing for people. She knit mittens and sweaters, did some baking—everything she could think of to earn some money. I knew, too, that she did these inside things because she wanted to stay home with me—for me.

"Yes, Mutti, I think I understand." It was all I could think of to say. What was coming next, I wondered.

I watched my mother lower her head and stare at her feet. When she looked up at me again, her face was strained. I knew that look well. She was about to tell me something I wouldn't want to hear. My heart pounded. My feet were icy cold.

Mutti took hold of both of my hands and held them tightly. "Lizbeth," she began, all in a rush, "this means you'll be alone at night, and I'll be sleeping a lot of the time during the day. I'd worry myself to death."

She stopped, took a deep breath, and then hurried on. "So I've made arrangements for you to stay in a place where you will be safe."

Mutti opened her arms to draw me close, as she often did, but I felt myself go stiff. It wasn't just my feet, now, that were cold, it was all of me. I stared at Mutti, without really seeing her.

"What kind of a place?" I asked, in a whisper.

"Well," she said and reached in her pocket for a handkerchief. She wiped her eyes, and folding her hands like she was saying a prayer, looked straight at me. "It's a——it's an orphanage, actually. But Pastor Karl says it's really a fine place, run by the church. And—and the children there are happy and well taken care of."

My insides trembled. I didn't believe what I had just heard. Away from my mother, for the first time in all of our lives together. Taken away to an orphans' asylum, a terrible place, I was sure. Even the name was terrible. I couldn't believe my very own mother could do this to me. I couldn't think of a single thing to say. I couldn't move.

"Please, Lizbeth," I heard my mother say, sounding far away, "try to understand. Please try to be brave."

Mutti stood up, and kissed me on the forehead and went into our tiny kitchen to fix supper. She left me alone with my pounding head and mixed-up thoughts.

I couldn't swallow a bite, and Mutti didn't press me to eat, or talk. We just sat in silence at our small table with its tattered oil cloth cover.

It wasn't until bedtime that the silence was broken. When I'd put on my nightie, Mutti brought me a glass of milk, tucked me in, lit a small candle as she always did, and started our bedtime prayer, "Now I lay me down to sleep— "

That's when I sat up, threw my arms around my mother, clung to her and started sobbing like a baby.

"Please, please, Mutti," I begged, the words pouring out in one breath, "don't send me away. I'll be fine alone. I'll lock the door when you're gone. And who would climb up three flights of squeaky stairs to get to me anyway. And anyway, how can I leave you alone? We've been together forever and ever. I don't want you to be alone in this big city. I don't!"

"I'll be fine, Lizbeth, really. And I can come Sundays to see you. It's only a short train ride, in a small town, southwest of here. And you'll be with children your own age. Some have no parents or relatives at all. Some come from broken homes, and have only one parent."

We both got quiet again as we always did when Mutti said things like that, reminding me I didn't have a father. I could tell the story by heart, I'd heard it so often. I was born in Germany right in the middle of the Great World War. My mother and father decided that when the war was over they would leave Germany and come to America. They wanted me to grow up in the "land of the free and the home of the brave." Their plan was that mother would come on ahead and get started here as a midwife, delivering babies. My father would stay in Germany to sell what was left of their home and business and then join us. But then, he'd died, and she had to come here with me, alone.

I looked at my mother now, trying to really see her. I saw lines in her beautiful face, a droop to her mouth. There was so much about my mother I didn't know, and until now hadn't thought to ask.

"Mutti, why couldn't you be a midwife here? Wouldn't you make more money that way? And we could stay here together. And be happy."

Mutti had explained this to me before, but I never really understood. Now she took a deep breath, and repeated the story as patiently as if she hadn't told me.

"It was terribly disappointing for me to learn that in this country you were not always free, and we certainly had to be brave. There is a law here. Only men with a medical degree can deliver babies. When I learned that, I thought my heart would break. It was so unfair. I was trained by the state in Germany. I knew I was good at it and I loved it so much—being with women during childbirth—comforting them, even saving lives sometimes. I—"

She couldn't go on, and I didn't feel like asking more questions. I knew she needed, and wanted, a steady job, but that didn't mean I wanted to go live in an orphanage.

In the days before Mutti's job began, we'd shed some tears together, and we argued, too, but Mutti wouldn't budge. All of my arguments, none of my tears, did any good. And that's how it happened that on this gloomy day, I found myself with my mother on the steps leading up to an orphan's asylum.

Rain had fallen all last night, but this dark day dampness still clung to everything. Mutti and I sat there sat there on those hard, cold steps, saying nothing for a long, long time. Finally, my mother stood up, pulled me up beside her and hugged me tight.

"Lizbeth," she said, "I have no choice. If anything happened to you while I was away at work, I'd never, ever get over it. Try to understand. Be brave. Your father would be proud of you."

My father, my mysterious father. All I had of him were dim memories. I'd never hear his deep male voice, telling me how brave I was, how grown up I was becoming.

I stood there, without a word, looking at my mother. There was sadness in her eyes. She looked drawn and so very tired. All the losses in her life, all the struggle. I knew in that silent moment, that I couldn't let my mother down, or my dead father either. I loved them too much, so I made up my mind. I would go to this horrible place for a little while and try my best to get along. I let go of my mother's hand, kept my eyes away from the dreadful, black sign that had taken my courage away, Central Orphan's Asylum, and we started up the stairs together.

CHAPTER II

WE REACHED THE top of the stairs without saying another word. My heart was still beating as though it would run away with me, but I stood beside Mutti without taking her hand. I would try to be brave, even though this was the worst moment of my whole life.

The only cheerful thing about the day was the cherry red coat my mother had made for me. It had a grey squirrel collar and a hat to match. I thought it was pretty spiffy and it was the only new thing I owned. Everything else was hand–me–down, from church folks. I pulled the soft fur collar against my cheek for comfort.

Mutti pressed on the latch and pushed. The door opened with a hollow sound. I looked down a long, dark, empty, hallway. It smelled like medicine, that made it hard to breathe. Mutti said it was sweeping compound and that meant the place was clean. All I heard was the ticking of a clock that hung on the wall. Its tick-tock sounded loud in the silence. Where were the happy orphans, I wondered.

Next to the clock were huge pictures in gilt frames—a man and a woman. Both faces stared straight ahead, not smiling. The man had a handle-bar moustache and looked to me like the German ruler, Kaiser Wilhelm. Underneath his picture was a brass plate with a name on it: Gottlieb Gerhardt Gastmann, Superintendent. 1866—. Still living, I guessed.

The woman wore a bonnet tied under her chin. She had a sad face. Her label read: Emma Wernecke Gastmann, Mother, 1858–1924. Dead, then, I supposed.

At the end of the hall was a door with a sign on it:

Superintendent. Mutti knocked softly. No answer. Then the sound of a chair scraping across a floor and the door opened. There stood a little man with bushy hair and a moustache exactly like the Kaiser's. One hand was behind his back. The other held a pair of glasses.

"So," he said, "You must be Frau Ebers, *ja*?" And this is—ah—Lizbeth—our new resident. Come in, come in. I'm Gottlieb Gastmann."

I recognized him from his portrait on the wall. He hurried us into his office, making a flat chuckling sound as he walked. "Everyone calls me Father Gastmann," he said. It sounded to me like we were supposed to think the children loved him a lot, but I wondered. I didn't like his moustache which hung down over his mouth, and I didn't like the frown lines on his face. And I especially didn't like his thick German accent. Hearing him talk reminded me of all the teasing I got at school for my own accent. Mutti and I had worked and worked together to get rid of ours.

Father Gastmann saw us looking at the photo on his desk—the sad-faced woman whose picture which we had seen in the hall.

"That is Mother Gastmann," he said. "My wife. Departed. We started Central."

He cleared his throat, ran his fingers through his thick hair, and went on talking as though Mother Gastmann was someone he didn't want to talk about.

"We have one hundred sixty children here," he said. "Most of them from broken homes—not strictly orphans, *ja*?"

He said things in his thick German accent like he was asking our opinion, but he wasn't really asking, he was telling. He didn't wait for us to answer him. Listening to his raspy voice, my bravery began to slip away and my legs began to feel watery again. I wanted to reach out for Mutti's hand, but I didn't let myself.

"Some were born," he went on, "—uh—out of wedlock, you understand, and—uh—the church takes care of them. Who else will? They'd be out on the streets if we didn't. *Ja*? We give them good food. Shelter. We run the asylum on good Christian principles."

"Come," he said abruptly. "I show you around."

He didn't wait for questions and Mutti was very quiet. Suddenly, I had to go to the toilet.

"I take you to the gymnasium first," he said, straightening his shoulders, "where the children play when the weather is not good. We believe in exercise. Healthy. Good discipline. Now we go."

Father Gastmann opened the door to the gym and a blast of sound hit my ears so loud I couldn't have heard firecrackers going off. Hundreds and hundreds of children, it seemed to me, were yelling and screaming in high, screechy voices. They were sliding down slides, jumping up and down on mats, twirling on parallel bars. I'd never seen so many children in such a small space in all my life, or heard children making so much noise.

Now I really had to go to the toilet. I wanted to turn my face into my mother's body, but I wouldn't let myself. That's when I looked up and saw the girl looking down at me.

She was sitting on top of the horizontal bar and was about my age, I guessed. Her arms were straight, her elbows tense. She was ready to dip down and swing all the way around. Her black eyes glittered as she looked down at me and she held her head high like a queen on a throne. She glared at me for a long time. If she had a name, I thought it must be Hatred.

Then, she tightened her grip on the bar, let out a wild yell, "Yippee," and let go!

Down and around she flew, a mop of messy black curls flipping and flying round her face. When she finished her swing, she sat on top of the bar and looked down at me again. She pressed her lips together, lifted her chin, and dropped like a bird on to the mat below.

Beautiful, I thought, in spite of myself. Beautiful—and free!

What makes her stare at me with such a mean look, I wondered. I was just standing there beside my mother, pressed close to her because she'd soon be leaving, because we'd never been separated, even for a single night, in all my life and I was getting so scared I couldn't breathe.

And now, to have one of these—these—orphans look at me like that! I didn't think I could stand it.

What was it she hated about me, I wondered. I was so plain. Straight, thin hair, the color of dishwater, skinny legs, squinty, washed out eyes that really needed glasses. The only pretty thing about me was my red coat.

I couldn't understand that girl, but I couldn't take my eyes off her.

Father Gastmann looked up when he heard Hatred yell. She was louder than all the other children in the gym put together. She sure wants us to look at her, I thought. What kind of children lived in this orphan's asylum, anyway. How could I possibly live with Hatred?

"That's—that's Georgiana," Father Gastmann hemmed and hawed, "comes from—uh—her mother is—was—" He took a deep breath and then finished in a rush. "Georgiana is a—a wild one! Needs watching—needs—uh—discipline."

He smiled, I think. I couldn't tell, because his moustache covered his mouth. I got the heebie-jeebies when I looked at him, smile or no smile. How could the children call him "Father?"

"Well, Miss Lizbeth," Father Gastmann went on, clearing his throat with a deep grumble, "shall we move on? We have more of Central to see before your mother leaves."

Mother leaves—that's what he said.

All at once I felt like a dark river was swirling over me. My heart thumped against my stomach and I hung on to my mother as we followed Father Gastmann out of the gym. At least for now I'd be away from the angry eyes of Hatred.

Father Gastmann led us back down the hall to some stairs. I had to go to the toilet worse than ever, but I couldn't ask where it was in front of Father Gastmann. Maybe Mutti would ask when we got upstairs. There had to be one up there.

When we got to the top, it was very quiet. So different from the gym. Father Gastmann knocked on a door and pretty soon it opened a crack.

"Oh, Father Gastmann, it's you," a woman whispered.

The door opened wider and we stepped into the first sunny room I'd seen so far.

The walls were pale yellow. There were plain, light colored curtains at the windows and bright pictures on the opposite wall. Below the pictures were cribs with sleeping babies. Babies in an orphan's asylum. Somehow I'd never thought of that before. Some of the cold inside me thawed a little.

My mother came alive. "Oh, my," she said. "A beautiful nursery. Now, I won't feel so bad about leaving Lizbeth."

The woman turned her plump body so we could see a baby's round moon of a face, eyes closed, mouth pink and open like a snap dragon blossom. Now I could see all of the lady holding it. She had dark hair that had a reddish shine to it. It was braided neatly and pulled around her head like a little crown. She smiled and her eyes crinkled at the corners. She was kind of round looking all over.

"This is Tante Anna," Father Gastmann said in his heavy, loud voice like the baby wasn't even there. Here we are using German words, I thought. Tante meant aunt. At least something was familiar.

Father Gastmann bowed a little quick bow in Mutti's direction. "Tante Anna, this is Frau Ebers. Her daughter Lizbeth here," he said. "Lizbeth is going to be with us because her mother works," he said, pouncing on the word 'works,' in the city. "She'll come Sundays. Uh—when she can, *ja*?"

Father Gastmann was in a hurry to leave, so we followed him out the door.

At the top of the stairs, I heard Tante Anna's voice call out in a loud whisper. "Father Gastmann, show the ladies where the girls' toilet is, *bitte*. Please."

With her free hand, she waved at me and smiled like we shared a secret. I already liked Tante Anna very much.

When we walked outside, everything looked soggier than it had before—sky, ground, buildings. It looked like the sun was never going to come out again.

The time was getting closer when Mutti and I would have ~~to say~~ to say good-bye. I wanted to get it over with. I didn't want it to come at all. These mixed-up feelings made my feet stick to the wet sidewalk as we walked to a new looking brick building, the place Father Gastmann said I would be staying.

He walked ahead, shouting back at us like he was giving a speech. "We start the cottage system. Cottages for ten, twelve orphans, with father and mother for each. Like a family, *ja*? So far, one cottage, forty orphans. No more funds. One hundred twenty in the Big House. Too many, *ja*?"

This was going to be my family? Forty brothers and sisters and over a hundred more in the Big House? And me an only child? Until now. I hung on to my mother's arm as we hurried along.

At the brick house we met a pointy-chinned lady named Miss Schlabaker. She was tall, thin, and had a mouth that looked like she'd eaten a sour pickle. She was in charge here. Did the orphans call her "Mother?"

Father Gastmann said good-bye, God Bless, in a hurry-up way and left us with Miss Schlabaker. Without one smile she showed us around, first to the girl's dormitory, where ten cots were lined up along one wall and ten along the other. She showed us the cot that was going to be my bed. Mutti sat down on it and put her hand on the grey blanket. She was looking as pale and cold as I felt.

"You may put your things under the bed, Lizbeth," Miss Schlabaker said. "I'll take your coat and hang it in the front closet. You won't need it too often. If you haven't got a sweater, I'll get you one from the missionary barrel."

Taking off my coat and giving it to Miss Schlabaker was like taking off my skin. Mutti put her arm around me as we walked down the hall, Miss Schlabaker speech-making like Father Gastmann.

"The boys sleep in the boy's dormitory at the other end of the building," she said. "Here is my office." The door was closed.

Next to her office was another door, this one closed, too.

But Miss Schlabaker opened it to a parlor with, a sofa and two arm chairs. It reminded me a little of Tante Anna's nursery.

"You can say good-bye here," Miss Schlabaker said, and left us, closing the door behind her.

In that moment a scene in the flickers I'd gone to one time with Mutti came to me. A woman was trapped on a railroad track with a train coming. The woman was clawing the air and her mouth was open like she was screaming, but no sound came out, because there wasn't any sound in picture shows. That's how I felt.

The good-byes had to go fast. My mother needed to catch the train back to St. Louis.

Now, I couldn't think of anything to say. We had said so much before this day. I had no more questions and more pleading would be useless. So we just sat there, looking at each other. No tears. They'd all been used up. I stared at my mother's pale face, at the strange red spot on each cheek. She held a handkerchief to her face and coughed a few times. That was all.

A grandmother clock on a shelf struck five. In the distance a bell rang—clang, clang, clang—five times. Supper time at Central Orphan's Asylum?

My mother stood up, reached for me, held me close. Then, without a word or a glance, she turned and hurried out the door. It clumped shut behind her.

CHAPTER III

I STARED AT the closed door, unable to move. Did I scream "Help!" like the lady on the track? I don't know if I made a sound or not, but a knock on the door scared me and I managed to whisper, "Yes?"

Miss Schlabaker opened it, her lips pressed together.

"Lizbeth, your mother's gone."

I felt like flying at Miss Schlabaker and pounding her and yelling, "I know! I know, dummy!"

Maybe if I'd had my red coat on, I could have. Instead, I took a shaky breath and bowed my head. "I know," I breathed, real low.

Miss Schlabaker stood there, arms folded across her skinny middle. "It's time to wash up for supper. In half an hour. Come, I show you the washroom."

Shouts filled the hall. I followed Miss Schlabaker down some stairs to the basement. The voices grew louder and higher the closer we got to the washroom.

"Girls!" Miss Schlabaker shouted when we walked into the steamy room. "Quiet down! You know the rules!"

"It's Georgiana again, Miss Schlabaker," a big girl standing at the sink next to Georgiana whined. "She started it!"

"Did not!"

"Did tot! Did tot!"

Did tot, did tot? What did that mean? Did it go along with the hateful stare Georgiana fixed on her victim? This time it was not on me, thank goodness. It was like a curse.

I watched Georgiana bend her black, tousled hair over the faucet.

She's giving up, I thought, relieved. The yelling and screaming will stop.

Next instant Georgiana raised her head, cheeks puffed out like a balloon, and quick as a monkey, she spit a whole mouthful of water at her enemy.

"No supper for you, young lady," Miss Schlabaker ground out between her teeth. She grabbed Georgiana by the arm, twisted it behind her back and marched her toward the door.

"Don't care!" Georgiana spat, turning back to glare again at the tattle-tale. "I'd puke if I had to eat supper with that snot."

A resounding slap was the last thing I heard as Miss Schlabaker shoved Georgiana out of the room. Hatred's cheek was a blazing red.

There was silence in the washroom as the girls bent over their sinks, splashing a little water on their faces, wiping their hands on the roller towel. I copied what I saw the girls do, wondering what was coming next.

"New here, ain't ya," a tiny little girl with green eyes said. "Georgie gets us all in trouble. She's bansh. Slopbucket hates her."

"And we hate Slopbucket," another voice chimed in and giggles bubbled up all over the room.

Bansh? Slopbucket? Did tot, did tot! Was I going to have to learn a whole new language? I looked at the four toilets all without doors and prayed I would be the last one out of the washroom. In the city school, the toilets had doors. But then, this wasn't a school, it was an orphan's asylum. If I waited until everybody left, where was I supposed to go for supper? Not that I'd be able to eat when I did get there.

A tall, thin, older girl with a long wispy braid hanging down her back came to my rescue.

"I'll wait for you," she said. "My name's Evelyn. We were told you were coming."

The sun had come out from under a bank of clouds when Evelyn led me back to the Big House. It spread in golden shafts across the field and lighted the woods beyond. I wanted to run to them, hide in them the way I once could hide in my mother's arms and never come back.

Somewhere back in a deep place in my memory, I thought I saw woods and I thought I remembered my father carrying me on his shoulders and setting me down to pick berries. I thought I could hear them plop in my pail. The city had no woods like these so that that must have been back in Germany, before we came to America. Before my father died, before—. A grey cloud came down in mind. The memory was gone.

"Pretty sunset," Evelyn said as we walked along. "There's some real pretty places in the woods. Sometimes we go on picnics there. Not often. We're not supposed to go there unless the grown-ups take us."

I smiled up at Evelyn. She was soft and gentle, like Mutti. She wasn't one to be afraid of.

"Evelyn, what does bansh mean?" I managed to ask.

Evelyn laughed a little. "I'm not really sure, but I think Kat started it. She's Irish, and I think the Irish have a word like banshee, that I think means crazy. I don't really know for sure."

"Oh," was all I said.

"I know it must all seem strange, but you'll get used to it," Evelyn said. "It's not such a bad place. Tante Anna is real nice. She came to us just a little while ago, and we already love her."

"Will I, I mean, can't I be in the Big House with Tante Anna?" I asked.

" 'Fraid not. Not yet. When you're thirteen or fourteen and if you don't get in any trouble and you show promise, then you may get to help Tante Anna in the nursery."

"Never!" I thought. "I'll never stay here that long. I won't have to. My mother will take me back home with her, where I belong."

Evelyn and I walked on to the Big House without another word.

The smell of cabbage, the vegetable I hated most in the world, hit me when we got to the Big House door. My stomach knotted. The clang of pots and pans, the sizzling spits of food frying and the sound of lots of voices jangled my ears. Meal time with my mother had been so peaceful, with just the two of us.

A bell dinged. The voices quieted down. Father Gastmann stood in front of rows of long tables, pressing on the bell as if it were in a classroom. "We will now bow our heads in prayer," he said.

Everyone mumbled along with Father Gastmann and when the Amen was over, benches were scrapped back and one hundred and sixty children sat down and dug into the food in front of them as if they'd never eaten before.

Evelyn found an empty place for me between two boys at a table that had mostly boys. I looked around for Georgiana, then remembered, "No supper for you, young lady!"

"This is Leland Dorfer. Leland lives in our cottage, we've got to calling the Brick House," Evelyn said, pointing to a plump boy on my left. There was an empty space on the other side of Leland as well. If I hadn't been seated next to

Leland, he would have been sitting alone. "And this is Buster Calder," she nodded to the boy on my right. "He lives in the Brick House, too."

I managed to smile at the boys as I sat down. Evelyn left me there and sat across the room, at a table with some older girls. I wanted to hang on to her and sit with those older girls, but I wouldn't let myself run after her.

"Here, have a sap sandwich," Buster said, reaching into the middle of the table and handing me a plate with a stack of white bread cut in half. Then he handed me a glass pitcher with a dark syrup in it. "You can fill up on these."

Buster had dark, curly hair, deep, tanned skin, and long lashes on eyes that looked like black olives. He smiled, a big, warm smile and my heart thawed a little. He showed me how to spread the sap on the bread. Then he held his nose and pointed to Leland.

"Nobody wants to sit next to Leland," he whispered. "He stinks! Wets his pants."

That did it. I couldn't eat a bite of the cabbage and fried potatoes, but the sap sandwiches tasted pretty good. I could hardly swallow the blue milk.

There were ten boys at the table, all in different shapes and sizes. One was a redhead with freckles that blurred together all over his face. They all snickered, their mouths full, not looking at me. They kept shoving shoulders and kicking each other under the table, as if they shared some secret. Were they snickering at me?

"Your name Lizzie, Lizzie?" Buster asked, grabbing another half slice of bread.

"I don't have a nickname," I answered, remembering Mutti's fear I would be called Lizzie in this country.

"Well, you know," Buster went on, "Henry made a lady out of Lizzie!"

"I am aware," I heard myself saying, "that Henry Ford has made a better car than the one called a tin Lizzie. But that's not my name." Only defense of my mother could have made me so bold.

"I am aware," the redheaded boy said, pursing his lips in a prissy way and mimicking me.

The whole table of boys snorted and held their mouths so the food wouldn't spurt out. Buster ignored me after that. Leland had been quiet the whole time.

I thought mealtime would never end.

Their plates wiped clean with bread, the boys still sat, giggling and jostling. The bell tinged again. Father Gastmann rose.

"You may leave the table. But remember, line up at the door, size order, and leave quickly and quietly."

It took me longer than anybody to leave the table. I tried to find a place in the line between two children about my size, but the children tightened the line the closer I came to them. It was two boys from my table who finally let me in. One was the red head. The other—Leland. I'd have to stand next to stinky!

What would I do between now and bedtime, I wondered. Would there be a light somewhere so I could read? When would the lights be turned out so I could crawl into my cot, pull the covers over my head and let my tears pour out by the bucketful.

When we got back to the brick cottage, Little Green Eyes helped me out.

"You can stay in the parlor and read, if you want. 'Til the

lights out bell rings," she said. "I'm Kathleen. Kat for short. We're in the same class at school, I think. Sixth Grade?"

I couldn't believe it. Sixth Grade? This tiny person?

"You'll get used to it around here. Not bad most of the time. 'Cept for Slopbucket and Father Gashole! They give me the heebie-jeebies. School's next week. Public school. Kids from town are snotty, but school's not bad. Oh, and hey, I think yer red outfit is the cat's meow!"

Alone in the parlor, I wrote in my diary, but it was hard. Sometimes, if I was sad, I'd write a poem, but tonight, no poem came. I opened my book, *Pollyanna*, but the pages blurred. I just sat there, numb and empty of all thoughts.

After hours, it seemed, another bell sounded "ting, ting, ting" and I walked down the hall to the dormitory. The room was quiet. I guessed the girls were all asleep. A form hunched under the covers in the cot next to mine but the form didn't make a sound.

I pulled my suitcase from under the bed, put on my nightie, folded my clothes carefully and put them in the suitcase. I put the suitcase back under the bed and crawled in between rough sheets and pulled a scratchy blanket up over my head.

Now, now, down under the covers in the deep, black private space, I could let it all out. I tried not to cry out loud. But the harder I tried, the louder I cried.

I felt a firm kick on my leg and heard a fierce whisper, "Hey, cry baby, stop sniffling. Can't sleep!"

It was Georgiana, no doubt about it. Georgiana—Hatred, the wild orphan, would be sleeping in the cot right next to mine. The shock was too great for tears. I clenched my fist, stuffed it into my mouth and bit down on my knuckles. It was hours before I fell into a half-sleep.

CHAPTER IV

The weather had turned warm again and just a few leaves were starting to turn when school began. We walked from the Orphan's Asylum to school in loose bunches, the High School girls and little First Graders from the Big House walking together. All of us from the Brick House straggled along in another bunch. Some of the boys tossed a ball back and forth all the way to school.

I felt at home in school. The smell of chalk dust and cedar furniture polish and musty books was familiar and good. The work was easy, too. School in St. Louis was much harder than here. The teacher, Miss Robinson, was kind and easy on the boys, who kept shuffling and shoving and clumping and poking whenever they moved from one place to another. After a few days, she stopped calling on me too often for answers. She learned quickly that I probably knew most of them. The children in the city had called me "smarty pants" until I learned to be very quiet and not raise my hand.

Kat was in my class. She was so tiny, the teacher put her in the front row so she could see the board. The redheaded boy whose name turned out to be Clarence Pringle was in my class, too. Pringle–dingle, the kids called him, but he didn't seem to mind.

The teacher put me near the back, because I was tall. There was one girl taller than me. Georgiana! She sat in the next row right behind me.

We seemed to be stuck with each other, somehow. I could feel her presence, even if I didn't turn around. She couldn't sit still. She was more like the boys than like any of the girls in the class, squirming and fidgeting, paying attention to the boys, not to Miss Robinson.

Kat had told me that the girls from town wore pretty dresses with panties to match and had bows in their hair and that they mostly avoided us orphans. I didn't much care, strange to say, but I had a hard time thinking of myself as an orphan. I wasn't either one—an orphan or town kid.

At recess, I jumped rope and played hopscotch with Kat, watching Georgiana out of the corner of my eyes.

"Hey, Georgie," the boys, both orphan and town, called to her at recess, "how about pitching for us?"

She was strong and quick and her fierceness made the boys all want her in their games. Her voice rang out. She was like a magnet for me, even though for some reason I was afraid of her.

Since that first night, we'd barely spoken to each other. It seemed safer to me, I guess. Every night she watched me fold my clothes as neatly as I could and put them in my suitcase under the bed. When I had crawled under the blanket, she would flop down with a kind of grunt and turn away from me. I stuffed my pillow over my mouth to keep from sniffling.

Then came the day of the explosion. It was over Leland. From the first day, I noticed something different about Leland. He held his mouth open a lot and walked with his toes pointed in. He was slow at everything.

Walking to school one day, Kat whispered to me, "Leland's not quite right, you know," and she pointed to her temple and rolled her eyes.

I felt sorry for Leland. Something about him made me want to take care of him, like my mother would have done.

So when Miss Robinson took me aside and asked me to help Leland with his math, I felt relieved.

I sat down beside him and he smiled at me like I was his best friend. He was a little smelly, but not really bad. Miss Schlabaker made sure he went to school clean. Cleanliness was a big thing at Central.

Leland could barely hold a pencil, much less write. What was he doing in the Sixth Grade? Miss Robinson gave me a first grade book, and I did the best I could trying to explain that "one" was a number and not the name of my first finger. We both jumped when the bell rang for the end of the school day.

It was on the way home that the trouble started. Leland brushed against me and tried to take my hand. I clutched my books close so I wouldn't have to take his, but I slowed my walk so he could stumble along beside me.

The boys from the Asylum bumped up against Leland as they shoved past and almost pushed him off the sidewalk.

"Lady Lizzie's got a sweetie," they sing-songed. "Peepee Leelie! Peepee Leelie."

Mutti had often told me to ignore teasing when I got it—for my clothes, my accent, which I didn't have anymore, or for just being different, I guess. I tried now. I tried to walk on and pretend I didn't care.

That just seemed to make it worse. Henry Pringle, who was bigger and stronger than the others, slowed down until he was just behind Leland and me. Then he pushed between us, stuck his foot out and tripped Leland, who fell flat on his face.

I dropped my books and knelt beside the crumpled lump of boy, who whimpered like a helpless puppy. I was still kneeling there when I heard Georgiana's war whoop, as loud as when she dropped from the horizontal bar in the gym that first day.

"All right, Pringle, you're gonna get it!" she yelled. "Why don't ya pick on somebody yer own size?"

She lowered her head and charged, ramming into Henry's stomach, making a sound like a thumped watermelon.

Henry held his stomach and backed up. Georgiana doubled her fists and crouched over like a prizefighter in a newsreel I'd seen.

"Come on, Pringle-Dingle, dare ya!" she taunted.

Henry's freckles blurred together in his flushed face. His eyes got big as balloons.

No one was paying attention to Leland and me. The kids had formed a circle around Georgiana and Henry. I couldn't see what was happening, but I heard the scuffling followed by a smack. Then a boo-hoo. The circle opened.

There was Henry wiping his bloody nose on his sleeve and slobbering, "You're gonna get it, Miss Georgie. Wait'll Slopbucket hears. Or Gashole! You gotta fight, doncha, Georgie." He sounded almost sorry—sorry that Georgiana had to fight, sorry she had to get in trouble.

"Nobody's gonna tell, okay?" It was Buster. He put his hand on Henry's shoulder and they walked on.

"Unless it's you, Lady Lizzie, " Henry yelled at me.

I looked at Georgiana and she stared back. There was no Hatred person in her now. Only a look that said, "Dare ya!" She brushed her dusty dress with a few swift swipes, lifted her chin and walked away. Leland and I walked together back to the Asylum.

That night, in our side by side cots, I wanted to reach out and touch Georgiana and say, "Thanks!" But I couldn't. I didn't fear her quite so much anymore, but I lay awake wondering and wondering about this person. Who was she, really? Most of the time, she seemed wild and full of hatred. Today she was a girl who risked getting into trouble at school or Orphan's Asylum, to stick up for a helpless boy—and maybe even me!

I lay awake a long time without tears, full of wonder. Was Georgiana getting to like me a little? Where had Hatred gone? Had she shrunk inside a person who cared about other people? Maybe it was only Leland she felt she had to protect. I would never dare ask her, but I wanted to wake her, talk to her. I lifted my hand out from under my grey blanket and reached toward Georgiana's bed, slowly, slowly. But just as I almost touched her, she stirred, and I quickly pulled away. I turned my back to her, pulled my covers over my shoulders, closed my eyes, breathed deeply, and pretended to be sleeping.

A soft light coming through the window across the room bathed my face and I opened my eyes again to a flood of moonlight pouring into the room. Some of the children in the dormitory, breathed deeply. Some of them snored. A few nights ago, Kat had a terrible nightmare and woke up screaming. I'd sat up, wanting to comfort her, but Georgiana didn't even turn over. "Oh, lie down," she'd said. "She does that all the time." I lay back down.

Tonight all was quiet. Everyone seemed to be asleep. Then, I heard Georgiana stir. She got out of bed and tiptoed out of the room. The toilet, I thought. But she didn't come back for a long time, and I couldn't go to sleep with her cot empty. Where was she, I wondered. Where had she gone?

I was afraid to follow her, but couldn't stand not knowing.

What was this strange power she had over me, I wondered. I could see her raise her chin and say, "Come on! Dare ya!"

I got up out of bed and went to the wash room. That was safe. I could pretend I had to go, too. But Georgiana wasn't there. The hall was dark and empty. No use checking the outside doors. Miss Schlabaker locked us in at night.

The door to the parlor was slightly open and I could see soft moonlight falling on the floor. I pushed the door open a little wider, praying it wouldn't squeak. It didn't. I stayed close to the wall, hoping the darkness would keep me hidden.

A shadow fell across the floor, a bulky moving shadow, but with slim arms and graceful shadow fingers that waved and turned, moving closer and closer to the middle of the moon path. I held my breath as the figure casting the shadow moved fully into the moonlight.

It was Georgiana, dancing in the moonlight, but a different Georgiana from the fighter of the afternoon. Her fists uncurled like flower petals instead of doubling up ready for a fight. I watched her move silently, now bending down, now raising her arms and stretching them wide, her head bent back, wild hair swinging and swaying, finger shadows delicate as a woodsprite's in a fairy tale. She was under a spell, dancing—dancing to a music I didn't hear. And I was under a spell, watching.

Neither of us heard the footsteps coming down the hall. The click of a button broke the spell. The moonlight was gone. There, in the harsh electric light stood Miss Schlabaker, faded flannel bathrobe pulled around her, shock and anger on her face. How could she have known we were here? Did she stay awake all night, every night, listening for the smallest sound from any of her orphans?

"Georgiana!" Miss Schlabaker yelled. "What are you doing! What on earth do you think you're doing?"

Georgiana froze, as though she'd been put under a different kind of spell. My hand flew to my mouth, covering it, holding back the gasp that came from seeing Georgiana in that bright awful light. She was standing there barefoot, looking trapped and helpless for the first time since I'd met her. And she was wearing my red coat.

Miss Schlabaker clenched her fists and started toward Georgiana, looking angrier than she had in the washroom that first day. I remembered the sharp slap, and Georgiana's fierce shout, "Don't care!"

I didn't wait. I flew to Georgiana and stood in front of her, hardly knowing what I was doing.

"I told her she could, Miss Schlabaker. I told her she could borrow it anytime."

A lie. Why did I tell it? I'd never scared myself quite so much in my life. Miss Schlabaker narrowed her eyes, jaw muscles bunching up.

Behind me, I heard Georgiana stir, heard the plop of my red coat on the floor, heard Georgiana slip away, out the door, leaving me alone with Miss Schlabaker.

She looked at me without a word, but like she didn't for a minute believe me.

"She's a bad influence on you, Lizbeth," she finally said. "Get to bed! Georgiana knows the rules. You're still learning them. But I'll have to speak to your mother about this when she comes."

She stood at the door to watch me leave, then turned out the light. I could feel her eyes burrowing into my back as I walked down the hall to the dormitory.

Georgiana was curled away from me as always. I crept into

my cot and stared at the ceiling. This weekend was Mutti's visit. What would she say when she learned that I'd lied to cover up for Georgie? What would she think of Georgiana "borrowing" my red coat? Why had I risked hurting Mutti and being punished myself to protect a girl who hated me? So many questions whirled around in my mind, so many troubling thoughts and feelings. But this night, I didn't cry.

CHAPTER V

MY JOY AT seeing my mother again made me forget that Miss Schlabaker would tell her that Georgie was a bad influence on me and that I'd lied to cover up for her. My mother was with me again and everything was hunky-dory, as Kat would say.

Mutti looked pale and her eyes had a kind of glazed-over look. But her arms were filled with packages and her smile was even dearer than I remembered. Miss Schlabaker let us meet in the parlor and she held me so close I could hardly breathe.

We talked and talked. She wanted to know everything and so much spilled out that I thought I couldn't stop. I told her about Kat and Evelyn and the boys and school. I skipped over Georgiana, although I didn't know why.

I unwrapped the packages, one by one. There were mittens she had knitted for the winter ahead—a little early, I thought, but then, who knew when I'd need them. There were used sweaters she'd picked up at the Salvation Army. "So you won't have to use the missionary barrel ones," she said. "Some other children may need them."

The last package was stiff and thin. A book! I could tell. I unwrapped it carefully, my heart pounding. This was better than Christmas.

There it lay, on my lap—the most beautiful book I'd ever seen. The cover was a rich brown with golden swirl designs and gold leaf edges. I opened it. It was printed in German script and had beautiful pictures, each one covered with tissue paper. The title page said, *Immensee*, "Bee's Lake" in English, written by Theodore Storm. It was my mother's favorite story, one she had told me over and over. I fingered the pages, one by one.

"Oh, Mutti!" That was all could think of to say.

Mother reached over and kissed my forehead. "I found it in a second hand book store. I don't want you to forget how to read German. It's not against the law, anymore. Now that the war is over."

We both laughed a little and wiped our happy tears. It was time for the last package, the biggest—a huge box of homemade cookies for me to share. One hundred and sixty cookies—one cookie for each orphan. Mutti must have baked for hours and hours, hours stolen from her sleeping time.

I felt like heaven had come to Central Orphans Asylum. My mother stayed the whole weekend. On Saturday Tante Anna joined us and the two of them seemed like old friends, my mother tall, thin and pale, Tante Anna short, round and rosy. Together they taught some of the girls how to darn stockings. My mother told them stories about her experiences delivering babies in Germany—how she had gone through the dark forest by sleigh to get to the expectant mother, how brave the women were.

Mother's pale face glowed when she talked and the red spots on her cheeks deepened. She coughed several times, took out her hankie and then went on. The girls asked lots of questions and their eyes widened as they listened. Tante Anna listened as intently as the girls and shook her head when Mother said she couldn't practice midwifery here in America.

"Does it hurt much—having a baby, I mean," Kat asked, her voice squeaking with excitement. Miss Schlabaker had been coming in and out of the dormitory, checking on us, I guess. Her expression never changed. Mother waited until she left this time before she answered.

"Sometimes very much, Kathleen," she said, calmly, "depending on how the mother is built. But there is much we can do to help. And when the birth is over and the mother holds her newborn lovingly in her arms, all is forgotten."

She smiled at me and I thought I'd burst with pride. I looked at Georgiana who hadn't asked a single question. She wasn't looking at my mother, but was picking at a hole in her stocking. She hadn't joined in the darning lesson either.

Saturday passed quickly. Sunday came.

Sunday dinner at the Big House was special—meat loaf, mashed potatoes—and jello. Mother chatted comfortably with Buster and Clarence and paid special attention to Leland.

The best part was when Tante Anna and her husband Onkel Chris came over to the table to greet Mutti. They often came for Sunday dinner with the orphans. They usually sat with Father Gastmann. He was a different person on Sundays with Tante and Onkel.

Onkel Chris was very tall, towering over the other grown-ups. His hair was starting to turn silver and he had a deep bass voice. He often sang for us and led us in songs like, "*Ich bin ein Musicann*," meaning, "I am a musician," and he taught us how to make sounds like musical instruments "Boom-boom here, squeak-squeak there" and we all laughed and laughed, it was so funny—one hundred sixty voices making silly sounds. Even Father Gastmann laughed. Even Miss Schlabaker tittered.

He would sometimes give little talks that we could all

understand and recite poetry like, "If you can't be a pine on top of the hill, be a shrub in the valley below—"

I was sure that if my father had lived, he would look and be like Onkel.

All during my mother's visit Georgiana kept to herself, sitting at the edge of the circle. I was so happy to see Mutti and was so proud of her that I forgot Georgiana and my red coat, forgot the lie, forgot that my mother would have to leave Sunday afternoon. I hardly noticed that Georgiana was quiet—not like her usual self.

It was during the time alone before Mutti left that she mentioned Georgiana—and the lie.

We were reading from *Immensee,* taking turns, Mutti translating parts I had trouble with. She got to the end of Chapter II and slowly closed the book.

"Tell me about the dark, curly-haired girl whose cot is next to yours. Georgiana, Miss Schlabaker called her?"

My heart started to thump. "Well,—she's—she's a little unruly—and has a terrible temper—but she's really nice—underneath."

"You like her, don't you?" Mutti's voice was soft.

I nodded and hung my head. "She reminds me of the gypsy girl in *Immensee.* You know, the one Reinhardt wants to go away with?"

"Yes," my mother said. "I can see that. Wild and wonderful. But you know what's right and what's wrong, don't you, Lizbeth."

That's all Mutti said about Georgiana dancing in my red coat and about my lying to protect her. Mother took her handkerchief out of her purse and coughed, face flushed. She stood up.

"I must leave now, Lizbeth. I'm not sure when I can get back. But as soon as I can. I understand from Fraulein Schlabaker that you are doing just fine. I'm glad."

We hugged each other again and without any more words, my mother turned and left.

I held the tears in when Mutti left, wanting with all my heart to be brave for her. But when I finished getting ready for bed, I curled down in my safe place under the covers. I turned away from Georgiana and held myself tight to keep from crying.

Soon, though, I felt a firm kick on my bottom.

"Miss your Ma?" Georgiana hissed.

I didn't answer.

Georgiana went on in a secret-sharing voice. "I don't have a ma like yours. Mine's a gypsy. Moves around a lot. The tribe comes in the fall and in spring and camps outside town. When they come this time, I'm gonna run away and join 'em."

I held my breath. This was this first time in all these weeks Georgiana was talking to me. I had to keep her going.

"What about your father," I asked, wondering about mine.

"Dead. Died in a fight. Stabbed. He woulda won, but he tripped on a tree root."

It all seemed so strange—Georgiana, a gypsy! Thoughts and memories banged around in my head—Mutti's love of *Immensee,* my fascination with the story's gypsy girl, Georgiana's dancing in the moonlight wearing my red coat, Mutti's leaving. Where was Georgiana's mother? What really happened to her father—what really happened to mine? What did he die of?

Georgiana's voice cut into my swirling thoughts. "Guess

what," she was saying. "The gypsies come through in the fall, too. When they come, I'll take you to their camp. If you want. It's off in the woods."

The woods—those woods that called to me so strangely and stirred dim memories. Memories of sounds filled my ears—birds calling, wind whistling, a grown-up voice way above me. My father's? Was it my father's voice I was remembering? Did my father take me for walks in the woods when I was so small that his face was way up above me, nearly touching the sky? Did we pick strawberries together like Reinhardt and Elizabeth in *Immensee*? An ache filled my heart, a longing I couldn't find a name for. Those memories seemed so unreal, more like fairy tales, or part of *Immensee*. Part of me wanted to slip back into those woods right now and go find my father.

But another voice called me back, a voice solid like a tree rooted in the earth.

"Hey, Lizzie," the voice called, "doncha wanta come with? Doncha dare?"

Georgiana, alive, real, and in the cot next to mine, was inviting me in to her secret life, into the woods that held so much mystery for me. Now I had more reasons than one to follow her, and nothing could stop me, if only I dared.

CHAPTER VI

MUTTI USED TO call them "dwindle-days"—that time of year when the days got shorter faster and the leaves turned beautiful colors. Almost overnight, they let go and started twirling down. The nights were cool and crisp and the days warm. Indian summer, the Americans called it. Mutti said the forests in Germany didn't turn such beautiful colors as here. And seeing the woods at the edge of Central and on the sides of the streets on the way to school made me almost happy to be in a small town at the edge of the woods.

School was going pretty well, too. I was making progress with Leland and arithmetic. I picked up acorns on the way to school and used them instead of fingers to help him learn to count. Leland was a gentle, friendly boy and I was proud of how well he was doing. The other boys were teasing him less, too.

At school, I still didn't have much to do with Georgiana. I stayed with Kat and some of the younger girls at recess and we jumped rope and played hopscotch and "still-light." Georgiana stayed with the boys, shooting baskets, playing softball—doing boy things. I watched her slide into base, hair flying, underwear showing. She didn't seem to mind. She would have been better off in pants, I thought, like the boys; but of course, that was impossible. No one at school knew how graceful she could be. They hadn't seen her dancing in my red coat.

It was at night, after the lights were out, that we talked, in whispers, so we wouldn't keep the other girls awake.

"The gypsies oughta be comin' through soon," Georgiana said one night. "They dance and tell fortunes and sell pots and pans and things. Town folks don't like 'em. Say gypsies steal and are dirty and break the law all the time. I think they wish they were gypsies. Free, you know. I think they're jealous."

"Could be," I agreed. That's when I started to tell her the story of *Bee's Lake*. It wasn't all that easy for me to read German anymore, but the book Mutti gave me was a children's version and I loved that book so much I was sticking to it. I thought Georgie would like it, too, partly because it had a gypsy in it. So I could hardly wait to tell her the story.

"There was this man," I began. "When the story begins, he's old and sad and he remembers when he was a little boy and there was this little girl that he went into the woods to pick strawberries with. They loved each other like little boys and girls do, and he wanted to marry her when he grew up. Her name was Elizabeth. I was named after her."

"Why doncha read it to me," Georgiana interrupted. "And I can look at the pitchers."

It was too dark to read that night, but I agreed to read to her after school the next day. We sat on my cot and I translated from the German as I went along. It took us days, while the daylight faded earlier and earlier.

When we got to the part where Reinhardt meets the gypsy girl, Georgiana got so excited she almost tore the tissue paper that covered the picture. There she was, a dark, beautiful girl, holding a zither and looking like she was saying, "Follow me!"

"That's ma," Georgiana said and got up on her knees, holding the picture up to the sunlight streaming through the window. "That's the way she looked. I know!"

"You're bansh, Georgie," came Kat's high little voice from across the room. "You ain't got a ma."

"Have, too," Georgiana practically shouted. "How much do you know!"

"I know 'cause Slopbucket told us we were all bastards 'cause our mas never married an' there's no place to go but here. Nobody wants us."

Georgiana shoved my beautiful book at me and started across the room after Kat. It was the first near-fight in weeks. My heart sank.

Evelyn stepped between the girls. "Kat. Georgie. Stop, right now. Miss Schlabaker will punish you both if you get in a fight. What Miss Schlabaker says is not that important."

Kat stuck her tongue out at Georgiana, who simmered down, looking more hurt than angry. I couldn't believe she gave up the fight so soon. But she liked Kat and maybe what Kat said was true. I closed *Bee's Lake* for the day and put it away in the suitcase under my bed.

That night, when everyone else was breathing deep, I felt the familiar kick on my leg. "It's true—my ma was a gypsy," came the fierce whisper. "I don't think she's dead. When the gypsies come, I'm gonna follow 'em and find her. Wanna come with? I dare ya!"

I didn't know if there were any gypsies. I didn't know if Georgiana had a mother. But I knew I would follow Georgiana into the woods. Every day, I felt more and more daring. Maybe there, in the woods, we'd learn about Georgie's past and I'd learn something more about my father.

The time came sooner than I would have believed. It was the balmiest day of Indian summer when the Gypsies came through. On our way to school we heard the far-off tinkling of bells and the clanging of pots and pans, more musical than the harsh noise of Central's banging kitchen kettles.

We waited with our mouths open, Kat and Clarence and Buster, Georgiana and me. Leland pushed up against me. One man was out raking leaves. Before the gypsies passed his house, he stopped raking and disappeared. A woman opened her front door, took her little girl by the arm, pulled her into the house and shut the door. Now, there were no townsfolk in sight. Only the few of us from Central Orphans Asylum were all that stayed to watch the gypsies appear. The only other person still on the street was our policeman, Mr. Schmidt, who walked up and down, swinging his club.

Soon the gypsies appeared, rattling down our dirt street, right in front of us. Some were riding in carts that had poles sticking up and everything you could imagine hanging on the poles, clothes and pots and pans and baskets and rakes and shovels and bunches of sticks. A few of the men rode horses. Some walked.

"Ain't they grand!" Georgiana whispered as we watched them straggle by, wagon wheels creaking. "Look it! Bright clothes, and all those earrings. Even on the men! And look it! A dancer!"

Sure enough, just between the last cart and the last horse, a young woman twirled in the dust with bare, brown feet, tapping and shaking a tambourine as she danced past us. She wore a bright red bandana on her head and bells on her ankles. The man on the horse behind her was riding bareback, playing a wild tune on a violin.

She danced right up in front of us, then stopped, suddenly, with a last tap on her tambourine. She fixed her wide eyes on us, but seemed to stare right through us. There was a glitter in those eyes that reminded me of Georgiana that first day I saw her, but there was no hatred in them, only a deep look, full of fire and magic.

She smiled then, the most dazzling smile I'd ever seen. Her teeth were so white, I thought she must have painted them. "Want yer fortune told?" she asked. "I'll tell it to yer for five cents!"

She didn't wait for an answer, but threw her head back, laughed, and shuffled along, swinging her hips, tambourine dangling and tinkling against her long, colorful skirt.

A few of the men glanced at us from under hats pulled far down over their eyes. One of them was wearing an earring! I couldn't believe it. None of the gypsies smiled, except the dancer.

"That's what I'm gonna be when I grow up," Georgiana breathed when the gypsies had passed us and were disappearing down the road. Her voice was full of wonder. "A gypsy. A gypsy dancer and fortune teller!"

"You're bansh," Kat squealed. "You said you already were a gypsy. And I ain't never seen you dance."

I didn't say anything. I waited for Georgiana to explode. But she didn't. She was calm, for once as she answered Kat. "I am a gypsy. Want me to prove it? Want me to take you to their camp in the woods after school and prove it?"

"The woods!" Buster hooted. "We're not allowed. We'd get the dickens!"

"So what!" Georgiana snapped. "Doncha dare?"

I felt a mean stab inside me. The green-eyed monster of jealousy, Mutti called it. Georgie was inviting everybody into her secret world. I wasn't special anymore.

"We'll be late for school," I said, turned my back on Georgie and the other kids and walked on, listening to the clanging and banging of the gypsy wagons growing fainter and fainter.

But the seed had been planted. The warm fall days would soon be gone. If I was ever to follow Georgiana into her secret world, now was the time. And maybe being in the woods would help me remember more about my father. I had to know if Georgie had been making it all up about being a gypsy. But where and when had she learned to dance? I had to find all this out, no matter what.

With that thought, I lifted my chin like I had seen Georgiana do many times and walked on to school with Leland beside me. I would take up Georgiana's dare, no matter who she brought along.

CHAPTER VII

WAS IT the warm, gold-colored fall afternoon or some kind of magic that drew Georgiana, Kat, Henry, Buster, Leland and me into the forbidden woods after school? Was it the gypsies casting a spell over us from a distance? Or was it Georgiana herself who pulled us into a circle around her like a magnet? I wondered about it afterwards, many times.

Whatever it was, we found ourselves bunched up around Georgiana, waiting for the rest of the kids from Central to wander back to the orphanage from school. Then we turned to our leader and waited.

"This way," she said, pointing in the opposite direction from the asylum and sounding more confident than I felt.

It was easy following the wagon tracks at first, but the road forked at the filling station on the edge of town. There, all kinds of wheel tracks from cars, farm wagons, tractors mixed up with those of the gypsy wagons.

"This way," Georgiana said, still sounding sure of herself and pointing to the road that led directly into the woods.

The road got smaller and smaller until it was no more than a trail. Then, it dipped straight down, onto a flat, treeless plateau covered with straw. Just beyond that space a muddy river flowed slowly along. It was wide but not as wide as the Mississippi, which I'd seen in the city. Still, it was too wide to jump across and too swirling to swim across, if any of us could swim, which I doubted.

If the gypsies had followed the trail to the river, how had

they gotten across? Where had they gone from here? I didn't see any sign of a trail on the other side.

"Hey," Georgiana shouted. "This is the ferry! See! That's what's the straw's for—to keep the cars and wagons from getting stuck in the mud. I seen it happen once at a Sunday school picnic, a long time ago. The gypsies drive their wagons over the straw, drive them onto the ferry boat, horses and all. And that's the way they cross river, doncha see? Come on, let's climb that hill over there and look for the ferry.

None of us questioned Georgiana as we crossed the straw-covered flat and started scrambling up a steep bank. The higher we climbed, the farther away from the river we were. When we reached the top, I looked down. Far below, the muddy water turned, flowing much faster than it had on the flats. My tail bone quivered. I had to look away from the river into the woods behind us. The sun was coming through what was left of the leaves, but the forest was not as open and light here as it had been when we started out.

"Hope ya know what yer doin'," Buster said, puffing from the climbing.

I hoped so, too, but didn't say anything.

"This way," Georgiana answered. "We're headed back to Central, anyway, even if we don't find the ferry."

We pushed on through the underbrush, faithfully following Georgiana. She took her time, acting like she sure knew what she was doing. She picked wild rose hips and nibbled them, and looked for ripe persimmons lying on the ground.

"Here. Taste," she said to me, holding out a squashy blob of orangeish fruit. "Come on, try it. They're puckery when they're green, but sweet when they're ripe."

I shook my head and Georgiana looked disgusted. "Some people," she said, "sure are 'fraidy cats."

Buster found some hickory nuts and cracked them open on a rock with another rock.

I watched the sunlight fade, worry growing inside me. Every one else seemed to be having a good time.

Kat started singing in her high, clear voice, "O Susannah, now don't ya cry for me. I'm goin' to Loosiana with my banjo on my knee."

I knew enough geography to know the rivers in this part of the state, emptied into the Missouri, and then the Mississippi, which flowed south. If we followed the river, maybe we would reach Louisiana—some day!

Kat was singing so loud, she didn't look where she was going and tripped, falling flat on her face. I helped her up. She wasn't singing anymore, but whimpered a little. "I'm gettin' tired, I guess, " she said.

"Me, too," Leland echoed.

"I'm hot and thirsty," Henry complained.

For the first time, Georgiana didn't have anything to say. No one did. It was getting duskier by the minute, and very quiet. In the silence, we heard a whippoorwill call from the woods across the river. When it stopped, it was quiet again. Then, faintly, far away, came the sound of rushing water.

"Jacobs Falls!" Georgiana yelled. "We're near Jacobs Falls where we picnic—once in a blue moon."

Thirst and heat and tiredness disappeared suddenly and everybody but me started sliding and tumbling down the bank towards the sound of falling water. I picked my way as carefully as I could, not wanting to tear my dress or scratch my legs.

At the bottom of the hill a small stream curled under some brown, overhanging ferns and the rushing sound was louder.

"It's the branch," Georgiana said. "The pool must be near."

She led us along the stream, sure footed and confident. Before we'd gone many steps, I was startled by a beautiful waterfall, spilling down some rocks and forming a pool that looked cool and bottomless. Below the pool was another, smaller waterfall and beyond that, the stream widened, turned brown again and flowed on.

At the edge of the pool, we all knelt down and drank from the quiet water.

Georgiana suddenly bounded up, pulling off her shoes, stocking, dress, and throwing them into the bushes. "Hey! Let's go swimmin'!"

I couldn't believe what happened next. Everyone—except me—hustled out of their clothes. Dresses, shirts, shoes flew everywhere. I held my breath. Girls in their panties was one thing. But boys without trousers! What if they took off their underpants. I'd never seen a boy naked in my life. I felt my face grow hot with shame—and fascination. I wanted to look away. I couldn't look away. In seconds, three pairs of trousers flew over my head and I watched, frozen stiff, as five practically naked orphans plunged and leaped into the pool, screaming and splashing water on each other.

Kat screeched with delight. "Come on, Lizbeth! Come on in!"

"Come on in, Lizzie," Buster and Henry shouted together, splashing water, trying to hit me with it. Leland blubbered and giggled.

Clearly, they'd forgotten the gypsies. This was exciting—free! Free from all the rules at school and Central Orphans Asylum.

I stepped back and almost fell into the hazel brush. I was hot and tired, too, and the pool looked inviting. But I couldn't move. Never in my life had I jumped into water like that. I'd taken barely warm showers at the orphan's asylum and had sat in an inch of barely warm water in a cold bathroom in the city, but that was all. This was scary, forbidden, against any rules I'd ever known. Jumping in a pool of water was bad enough, but jumping around, boys and girls together, with nothing on but their underpants was impossible, sinful, even.

I pulled back, hugging myself, and watched my friends prancing like horses and leaping like frogs, envying them all. Just then, Georgiana stopped and looked at me. Her eyes bored holes right into me.

"Dare ya, fraidy-cat!" she shouted and ducked her whole self under the water.

I didn't dare, even though I wanted to so much.

The sun shafts were paler and longer when everyone crawled out of the pool, shivering, and reached for their clothes. It was not only duskier in the forest, but it had suddenly grown chilly.

The way back to Central seemed much longer than the way into the woods. The trees seemed taller, the underbrush thicker.

"How far we go, Georgie?" Leland asked, voice trembling.

"It's gettin' dark," Kat whined. "I'm cold."

"I'm hungry," Henry complained, like it was Georgiana's fault.

"Are we lost?" Leland was crying now.

"Shut up!" Georgiana commanded. "I hear the supper bell!"

"You're bansh!" Kat spit out.

Georgiana ignored Kat and held up her hand. "Stop!"

We stopped and listened. The forest made no sound. But off in the distance we heard the faint clanging of Central's supper bell. For the first time since I'd come to the orphanage it sounded welcoming. We had no leader now. We all plunged toward the sound.

Light from the setting sun was gone when we reached the edge of the woods and stepped out into the open field I'd seen that first rainy day. It wasn't raining now, but that dreadful time came back to me as though it were yesterday. The forest had called me then. Maybe I'd thought that in the woods beyond the field, my father would rescue me. This afternoon, I hadn't thought about my father at all.

Everyone, except me, was wet. I looked at my friends, damp clothes clinging to shivering bodies, their hair a wet mess and felt a need to protect them all, like Mutti would have done—or Tante Anna.

We reached the sidewalk leading from the Big House to the Brick House, and started sneaking the rest of the way to change for supper. Just before we got there, two flashlight beams fell on our faces. We couldn't see who was behind those beams, but I knew, without a doubt, Miss Schlabaker, surely—and Father Gastmann!

A blurry time followed. I don't remember who jerked and shoved us up to the Big House, through the dining hall where the other orphans were eating their supper. The clink of forks on plates stopped as we were marched past the staring orphans and down the hall toward Father Gastmann's office.

Georgiana, Buster, Henry, Kat and Leland, shivering terribly now, were lined up in the dark space under the stair well. I was the last in line and the first to be taken by the hand and led into Father Gastmann's office by Miss Schlabaker.

Father Gastmann was sitting at his desk, hands folded on top. He peered at me over his glasses.

"Who led you into the woods, Miss Lizbeth?" he asked.

"I—uh—well—"

"It was Georgiana, was it not!"

"Well, uh—Lizbeth didn't get wet, Father Gastmann. She didn't go swimming," Miss Schlabaker broke in.

Father Gastmann ignored her. "Did the children take off their clothes?" he demanded.

"Oh, no!" I managed to say, wondering if I was telling a lie. "I mean—not all of them. I mean—not all of their clothes." I felt worse than a tattle-tale, remembering how I had not been able to take my eyes off the near-naked boys.

"So then, Miss Lizbeth, you, yourself, did not disrobe in front of the boys?"

"Oh, no sir!" I answered quickly.

"Hmm—" Father Gastmann twiddled his thumbs. "Well, then. You will not be punished. This time. You're still new. *Ja*? You'll go to bed without supper and you will stay away from Georgiana. She's a bad influence. Miss Schlabaker, see to it!"

He waved his hand to dismiss us.

I dared not look at my friends as we passed them, huddled under the stairs. I wanted to run back into Father Gastmann's office and yell, "Why do you pick on Georgiana? It's not all her fault. I wanted to follow her!"

But I didn't. I walked along beside Miss Schlabaker with my head down, went straight to my cot beside Georgiana's empty one and crawled in, clothes and all.

It seemed like ages before the older girls started coming back to the dorm. Nobody said a word. I pulled the covers over my head. I wasn't hungry, just sick to my stomach.

It was Kat's high squealing that made me peek from my hiding place. She was limping. Blood ran down the back of her legs and she sounded like a tortured kitten. Her tiny arms were clinging to the round body of Tante Anna.

Georgiana followed, chin up, jaw stuck out like she dared anyone to take a poke at her. Evelyn, the peacemaker, followed Georgiana, gauze and medicine bottles in her hands.

The scowl on Tante Anna's face was deep and dark. She helped Kat onto her stomach on her cot, took some salve and gauze from Evelyn and started to gently touch Kat's bleeding legs.

"This will sting, dear heart," Tante said softly, "but it will help."

Next to me Georgiana jerked back her covers and flopped down on her stomach. Blood ran from the switch marks on the back of her legs but she didn't make a sound. As she had during my first days at Central, she turned her face away from me.

When Tante Anna finished soothing Kat, she came over to Georgiana.

"Here, dear heart," she said. "Let me help you."

Georgiana, face buried her face in her pillow, shook her wild, wet curls and muttered, "No! I'll puke if you touch me. Go away. Leave me be!"

Tante Anna didn't touch her. She only murmured, "Alright, dear heart. As you wish. I'll come back later."

With that she turned to leave. She stood at the door, gauze and medicine bottle in her hand.

"Girls," she said, to all of us, "I promise you, if my life depends on it, you'll not be beaten again."

And she left the room.

When she was gone, Evelyn burst out, tense and excited, "She's a saint, I tell you!"

Questions bubbled up from all the girls at once. “What happened? Did the boys get beat up?”

Evelyn sat down on her cot, cupping her cheeks in her hands and rocked back and forth. “You should see the boys! Backs broke open with lashes from the razor strop. Blood all over their backs. They’ll have to lie on their stomachs for weeks. And you know what Tante Anna said to Father Gastmann? ‘How could you beat those children like that!’ she said. She sure was mad! And then he said, Father Gastmann said, ‘Those children are bastards, born in sin. You have to beat it out of them. That’s what the Good Book says.’ ”

Every girl in the room except Georgiana, Kat, and me mimicked the rest of Father Gastmann’s words in a sing-song chorus, “The sins of the fathers visit the children to the third and fourth generation.”

When they finished, Evelyn went on, “‘Suffer the little children to come unto me—for of such is the Kingdom of Heaven. That’s what the Good Book says to me!’ That’s what Tante Anna said.”

The room was quiet now. No one had mentioned me. I lay alone in my bed, longing for my mother. I asked no questions, didn’t say a word. Georgiana didn’t either. She just lay there beside me, bleeding and silent.

CHAPTER VIII

AFTER THAT THINGS were different at Central Orphan's Asylum. We did our Saturday chores of cleaning and changing beds, with a strain in the air. The kids barely spoke to me. I had the feeling everybody knew what was going on but me. They all seemed to be connected to a grapevine of information and I wasn't on it. I didn't see anything of the boys and I worried about them, especially Leland.

Kat's legs had stopped bleeding. They were covered with the gauze Tante Anna had put on, but she still limped and whimpered when she crawled in bed.

On Sunday morning I waited for her to dress before breakfast. "How's the boys," I asked. "How's Leland?"

She didn't look at me, but limped a little more. "Well, they ain't exactly hunky-dory."

On Sunday afternoon, during quiet time, I heard voices and the footsteps of some grown-ups shuffle down the hall to the boys' dormitory. When they shuffled back, all I heard was footsteps, no voices.

"Trustees," Evelyn whispered. "They really run the place. I bet Tante Anna called them to look at the boys' backs. To see for themselves."

"What if Tante gets in trouble!" Kat squeaked, and everybody gasped.

Everybody but Georgiana. She was still lying on her stomach with her face turned away from me. It was just like those first weeks, before we got to be friends. The only sound she made, the only words she had spoken to me since her terrible switching was a low muttering into her pillow that first night, “Germans is huns!”

What could I say? I'm sorry? I'm sorry you got switched and I didn't? I'm sorry I'm German? I'm sorry Mutti and my father and Tante Anne and Onkel Chris are German? But Father Gastmann—Gashole—what about him? What should I do—or say, I kept wondering. No answers came, so I wound up doing nothing, saying nothing. I kept silent and carried the heavy feeling in my heart, and pushed back the sting of the tears that wanted so much to pour out.

Evelyn was the only one who seemed to care how I felt. She walked with me to the Big House for dinner. She seemed to know what I was thinking, almost the way Mutti had.

“Kids get beaten a lot,” she said. “This was the first time Tante Anna had seen it. She hasn't been here very long. She won't get in trouble. Onkel Chris is a trustee.”

“But beaten so hard!” I said.

“It's hard to be responsible and control a hundred and sixty children, you know. You kids did scare him.”

“You mean he got mad because he was scared? Why didn't he just tell us he was scared?”

“Well . . . would that have made a difference next time somebody got a wild idea?”

In my mind, I saw Georgiana lift her chin and say, “I dare ya!” I couldn't think of an answer for Evelyn, but I wondered what Tante Anna and Onkel Chris would do if they were in charge. Or Mutti.

We walked on to the Big House. I forgot to ask her about Leland.

At dinner, Father Gashole was scowlier than usual and Slopbucket's lips tighter. They whispered together as they stood at the side of the tables, watching over us.

That night Georgiana still lay on her stomach with her face turned away from me. But she didn't say anything about Huns. She didn't say anything at all. I was going to have to start all over with her and all of the kids—and I couldn't imagine how.

I missed my mother again. I missed the father I couldn't remember. And I missed Georgiana, who was there and not there.

I thought things couldn't get any worse, but I was wrong. The very next day, after school, Slopbucket came into the dorm and told me my bed was to be moved—away from Georgiana, though she didn't say that. I didn't complain like I wanted to, but helped her move my cot and suitcase across the room between Evelyn and Edna, the chubby older girl Georgiana spit on that first day. Edna never said much at all, but she snored at night.

The day after that Slopbucket put her hand on my shoulder as we were lining up to leave the dining hall and kept me from leaving with the other kids.

When everybody had filed out, she said, "Father Gastmann wishes to see you."

I'd been scared and mixed up so often in these last months, you'd think I'd have gotten used to it. But I hadn't. Everything hit me so hard, the beatings, the kids turning their backs on me. All I could think of now was how fast I could get to the toilet. Was Father Gastmann going to give me the switching I missed before? It might make the kids feel better about me, but in my mind I could just see blood running down the back of my legs and I was terrified.

Miss Schlabaker pushed me inside Father Gastmann's office and closed the door.

This time his back was turned away from me. His hands were behind his back and he was looking out of the window. He took his time before he spoke. My heart was beating so hard, I thought sure he could hear it.

He cleared his throat. "Well, Miss Lizbeth, you've had quite an adventure, it appears. Ja?"

He turned around and looked at me. There was the tiniest glitter in his eyes. I couldn't tell what it meant, so I didn't say anything. I just nodded my head.

"Another of Miss Georgiana's ideas, I take it?"

Now was my chance—now, before he went on about bad influence and all that, I could speak out bravely and defend my best friend. I'd done it with Slopbucket, why couldn't I do it now?

I managed to shake my head a feeble 'no' but couldn't look him in the eye or say anything out loud.

"Miss Schlabaker tells me you have defended Georgiana before—about your pretty red coat. Ja? That's very kind of you and we commend you for it. But this is much more serious and it could get worse."

He cleared his throat and I managed to lift my head and look at him. What was coming next?

"The more you are together, you and Georgiana, the more influence she will have on you. There are other girls you can befriend—here in the Big House—a little older, perhaps, but nice girls. We haven't sleeping room for you here, but two of the girls are working in town, cleaning for townspeople. We've decided to let you take their place and help Tante Anna in the nursery when school is out. You'll like that, *ja*?"

What could I say?

"Cat got your tongue, Lizbeth?" Father Gastmann actually grinned. I wasn't sure what I was feeling, so I just shook my head again. Yes or no, it didn't matter what he thought I meant.

"Well, run along Miss Lizbeth. Tante Anna will be expecting you tomorrow after school," and he led me to the door patting me on the arm like I was a little kid.

When I thought about it that night, lying wide-eyed in my cot between Evelyn and snoring Edna, I wondered about some grown-ups—Father Gastmann, Miss Schlabaker. How could they put someone they said they cared about in such a mess? They knew how excited I'd be to work near Tante Anna. Everybody loved her. And I could help her with the babies. And learn from her, maybe. It was the best thing I could think of doing.

But what would my friends think—Kat and Clarence and Buster and poor dear Leland—and Georgiana—especially Georgiana. I remembered the look of hatred in her eyes that first day at the top of the horizontal bar when all I was doing was standing beside my mother in my red coat. Now, she had something to hate me for. I'd lost a friend—the only true friend I'd had in my whole long life.

Didn't grown-ups know how important friends were to people my age? And didn't they know giving me this privilege sooner than usual would only make them hate me more? Didn't they know a person couldn't make new friends over night—just like that?

Well, maybe I could stand being hated a little longer. I'd like being with Tante Anna and it could make the time go faster until Mutti would take me back home with her, where I really belonged.

Mutti! For the first time in my life, I wondered about my own mother. How could she make such a decision for me—leaving me in an Orphan's Asylum, feeling awful about being left and worrying, too, that I'd hurt her when I made such a fuss about it.

I'd just gotten to place where I didn't mind using the toilet without a door, helping Leland, getting to be friends with Georgiana. Until we got lost, it was special having an adventure with her and Kat and the boys. I'd just gotten to the point where I didn't cry at night and stopped tossing and turning before I went to sleep.

And now! I tossed and turned, turned and tossed. I punched my pillow. Finally, I went to sleep.

CHAPTER IX

EVEN BEFORE I started working in the nursery, word got around that I'd been chosen to work with Tante Anna. Before now, that privilege was only given to girls who had been here a long time and had earned it by being especially helpful in many ways. I thought I knew what the kids would think of my being singled out for this special treatment. But I didn't have any idea how awful it would be.

Neither Kat nor Georgiana would look at me, much less talk to me. At school I ate lunch by myself, taking one bite each of my sap sandwich and apple. I thought about going over and sitting with the town girls, but I took one look at them with their pretty dresses and decided it was too dangerous. I didn't want them to get that prissy look on their faces when they looked at my lunch or my hand-me-down dress. Just like in those first weeks at Central, I felt I didn't belong anywhere. I wasn't a town girl, and I wasn't an orphan either. I was a Nobody. I was outside of every circle of girls when they gathered in clusters around each other. I was all by myself, totally alone.

During recess Georgiana and Kat avoided me. One day I saw Georgiana lean down and whisper something in Kat's ear. I heard them use my name, and pretended I didn't notice what they said or did. Kat giggled and Georgiana laughed out loud. They were talking about me, making fun of me. I wanted to run far away, but where would I go? I wished the ground would open up and I could just disappear. I'd had this feeling before, in the city, where I was teased, or worse, ignored, for my accent, for my funny clothes, for me being "old for my age" as the teachers put it. But this was worse, because at Central we were like a family; and now, I was being pushed out of that close circle. And besides, back in St. Louis, I had Mutti to go home to, to comfort me and laugh with me.

The boys who'd been beaten weren't back at school yet. I didn't know how they felt about me or if they knew I hadn't been punished. I told myself I didn't care, but I was lying. Without Leland to help with his arithmetic, school was boring as well as painful.

Every day I waited for the bell to ring at four o'clock when school let out. I wanted to get out of there and go directly to the Big House without stopping by the Brick House. I could hardly wait to be with Tante Anna and her cheerful room full of babies and toddlers. That was the only place I was needed, and wanted, and had something useful to do.

Kat and Georgiana usually hurried out of school even before I did. Walking behind them, I couldn't help but see the red slashes on the back of their legs. They were healing, but still raw. I clutched my books tighter against me and walked on, trying not to cry right there on the sidewalk,

I was glad when I could turn in at the entrance to the Big House and leave Kat and Georgie going on to the Brick House ahead of me. The Big House didn't look as gloomy as it had that first day. I ran up the stairs as fast as I could.

"Well, dear heart," Tante Anna beamed when I came in the door. "How good to see you! Good to have more help. Here, put your books down and hold this baby."

I could have cried with relief and joy. I didn't know much about babies, but I knew Mutti loved them and I had loved playing with my baby doll before I got too old.

Before the first afternoon was over, though, I learned that

babies weren't exactly like dolls. For one thing, they were heavier. They wriggled and squirmed and fussed and messed their pants.

There were five babies Tanta Anna took care of and they all seemed to need attention at the same time. I was jiggling Baby Todd, trying to burp him like Tante Anna showed me and not doing very well, when who should walk into the nursery but Edna, the snorer. I was actually glad to see her. She took Todd from my arms and gave me a smile that said, "See, smarty pants, you don't know so much, after all."

Tante Anna stayed calm and patient and jolly when the babies' fussing turned into screams. She actually laughed out loud. "Poor dears, they're hungry. No wonder they're crying. They're in pain! And there's no warm breast to feed them. Warm the bottles, girls. Three of us will have to feed five babies."

In the middle of the week, someone knocked on the nursery door and when Tante Anna opened it, I saw Buster and Clarence and Leland standing there. They came to have Tante look at their backs and put on more salve. The nursery was also a nurses station and Tante was the Asylum's nurse as well as baby tender. I turned my back to the boys, so they wouldn't be embarrassed, and so I wouldn't have to see those beaten backs. I didn't want to meet their eyes, and they didn't look my way either. Buster and Clarence didn't make a sound. Leland let out a sad little "Ow!" I wanted to run to him, but I didn't.

"Put on your shirts, boys. Carefully. You can go back to school tomorrow. Your backs are healing nicely. Don't scratch if you start to itch."

After the boys left, we got busy again. Tante Anna didn't say anything. Edna didn't either. I certainly didn't.

By the time the weekend came, I was so tired, I couldn't sleep. I was still getting the silent treatment from Kat and Georgiana, and even from the girls in the Big House. It seemed to be getting worse each day. Once when I was walking up the aisle at school, Georgie stuck her foot out, trying to trip me. She snatched it back before Miss Robinson saw her. But the worst part was being ignored or whispered and giggled about behind my back. I wanted to crawl in a hole and just die.

If it hadn't been for the time in the nursery, I really think I would have died. I was learning a lot and it felt good to be doing something useful and feeling sort of important. I didn't mind Edna anymore and she showed me how to clean the babies' bottoms and pin clean rags on them, which we tore from old sheets. She wasn't ever mean.

And Tante Anna was a wonder. No matter how busy we were, she always stayed calm. Whenever a toddler waddled over to her, holding out its arms to be picked up, she'd scooped the little one up with a jolly laugh. My heart warmed as I watched her. She seemed more fun and loveable to me every day.

The days were fast getting shorter, and cooler. Sunlight came through the branches of the trees in long columns, like in a church. The trees and Tante Anna were the only good things about being at Central. The last few leaves crunched under my feet as I hurried to the nursery after school every day, trying to ignore the other kids.

I had an hour before Edna came when I had time alone

with Tante Anna. When the babies were sleeping or cooing in their cribs, she taught me Red Cross First Aid. She told me that she'd nursed returning soldiers during the Great War.

It was easy talking to Tante Anna and I told her all about Mutti's sadness that she couldn't be a midwife in this country.

Tante shook her head. "I can imagine," she said. "After all that training!"

I told her some of Mutti's stories about midwifery and some things I'd learned from her about childbirth.

"You know much more than most girls your age. You're lucky. You know," she said, leaning close to me like she was sharing a secret, "I wanted in the worst way to be a doctor. But it was unheard of, so I settled for being a nurse. My mother even thought it was unlady-like for me to be a nurse for grown-up men!"

She laughed her hearty laugh, "Well, now that we're not at war, I guess I'm happier taking care of babies. They need me here, and when the babies get sick, I can care for them. Unless it's very serious."

Love for Tante welled up inside me. I couldn't help it. I hugged her round, plump middle.

"Oh, Tante Anna," I mumbled into her warm body. "I love you. I love you and Mutti more than anything in the world. And I'll tell you something else. I'm going to be a doctor when I grow up!"

Tante Anna was quiet a long time, patting my knee. Then she said, "Dear heart, I hope you can do that. But it's going to take a lot of courage."

I thought I was getting some courage, cleaning babies' bottoms, rinsing the dirtied diaper rags, wiping their spit-ups.

And I thought I was getting used to the kids in the cottage treating me like I wasn't there. But at school and after I'd left the nursery I'd look at Georgiana and Kat and long to be friends with them again. Especially Georgiana.

And then, one night at bedtime, tired and lonely, I pulled my blanket back and tried to get in bed. I pushed at the sheet and couldn't get in. I pushed harder and heard the sheet rip. Someone had pulled the bottom sheet up to meet the top sheet, short-sheeting my bed. Everybody started laughing, even Evelyn. I wanted to cry.

Of course, Slopbucket heard the giggling and came in.

"Girls, quiet down! What's going on here!"

She looked all around, her glance lingering longest on Georgiana, whose glowing eyes looked wide and innocent as a kitten.

"My sheet tore," I offered quickly, "and it made a funny noise."

I may be a smarty pants and a goody-goody, I thought, but I'm not a tattle tale. Georgiana had to know that by now. Or maybe she didn't. Maybe she and the other kids think I told on them for running away and practically skinny dipping.

This time it was Evelyn who came to my rescue. "That's true, Miss Schlabaker. Her sheet tore."

Miss Schlabaker brought me another sheet. I changed my bed and climbed in.

The next day, there were dead flies in my lunch pail.

I needed so much to remember who I was—to remember that I was really not an orphan, that I had a mother who would come soon and take me away.

That was the thought that made me want to see my red coat again. I'd been wearing a heavy grey sweater from the missionary barrel, but now I wanted my red coat so I could pull its soft squirrel collar close and remember the mother who had made it for me. I hadn't worn it or even seen it since the night Georgiana danced in it.

I hurried to the hall closet after dinner, hoping no one noticed me. I opened the door and searched. My red coat was gone.

What could I do? It had to have been Georgiana who took it. Who else? If I asked the girls in the dorm about it, they'd deny it. If I asked Georgiana—the very thought scared me. If I asked Miss Schlabaker and got Georgiana in trouble again—that thought scared me even more. Now I had nothing. No friends, no red coat, no hope.

I crumpled. Not even the thought of seeing Tante Anna erased the pain inside me. I couldn't live with nothing but grown-ups all my life. I was beginning to feel close to Tante Anna, but I didn't feel ready to talk to her about all this either. There was no one I could talk to. All the lonely year ahead unrolled in my mind like a scene in a picture show. I saw myself walking to school all alone, crawling in bed at night, all alone, without anyone talking to me. There was no one I could laugh or share secrets with. How long was I going to ache inside like this? How long would I have to stay in this dreadful place?

These were the thoughts I had as I climbed the stair to the nursery the next day and opened the door. Across the room, sitting in Tante Anna's rocker and smiling like the sun coming up was my mother.

"Oh, Mutti!" I cried, dropped my books, and ran toward her.

CHAPTER X

FOR THE FIRST time since I'd come to work in the nursery, the few hours with my mother and Tante Anna dragged. Mutti and Tante acted like old friends. They talked midwifery, nursing, babies, not being able to be doctors. All the time they were talking, they kept busy with babies and bottles and blankets and diapers. Mutti wore a gauze mask over her face, which I thought was peculiar, but then she seemed to have a cold all the time. She and Tante talked to each other as though I wasn't there.

When the babies got quiet after being fed, Mutti removed the gauze mask from her face. Tante pulled the two nursery rockers close together and motioned for Mutti to sit beside her. They took out their hand work, Mutti knitting, Tante crocheting, both of them rocking and chatting. I stood beside Baby Todd's crib and jiggled it until he fell asleep. Watching them, I felt lonely all over again.

I was glad when the dinner bell rang and I could leave with Mutti and have her to myself. Everyone at the table seemed glad to see Mutti and talked to her as though nothing had changed.

Finally dinner was over and we walked back to the Brick House together and into the parlor. Now, at last, we were by ourselves.

"Oh, Mutti," I began and the story poured out. All of it. First, the search for the gypsies, the swim at Jacobs Falls, the way everybody but me got punished. I told her about everybody blaming me, hating me for not being beaten and for getting to work with Tante Anna.

I told her just about everything and it felt so good. The part I couldn't quite tell her was the short-sheeting of my bed, the flies in my lunch pail, the stolen red coat. I was sure these were all Georgiana's ideas and something in me still didn't want to tell Mutti.

"So you see, Mutti. I don't belong here! Please, please take me back home with you! We'll get along just fine. Just like we did before. I'll be safe. I'll lock myself in at night!"

I was out of breath. I was sitting on the floor in front of her, looking up at her, hoping she'd see how unhappy I was.

My mother sat very still and stroked my head. "I'm sorry you're so miserable, Lizbeth. Tante Anna told me. She told me, too, that things may change here. There'll be no more beatings. In time, the children will forget, Lizbeth, and you'll be friends again. Children forget easily."

Something brick-hard and hot set my heart thumping. I jumped up, glaring down at my mother. Words came out of me, like an echo, the same words I'd said when she first told me about Central, "Mutti! You're not going to leave me here? You can't! How can you? How can you do this to me—to—to—*us*!"

This time I didn't wait for an answer. I plunged on, spitting out, getting louder and louder.

"Mutti! I hate you! I'll die if you leave me here."

I ran out of the parlor and slammed the door.

In the washroom by myself, in the toilet without a door, I looked up and into the mirror above the wash basin. I didn't know the person staring back at me. Her face was red and blotched. I pulled down the skin below my eyes and stuck my tongue out at the ugly girl I saw. It had to be me. No one else was in the room.

Shame poured over me. Where did that ugly girl come

from? How did she get there? How could I have said those things to my very own mother? I was scared I would be punished for ever and ever by God Above. I washed my hands, splashed water on my face and asked our Father-who-art-in-heaven to forgive me and let my mother forget. I forced myself back to the parlor, hoping with all my heart my mother was still there.

She was. She was sitting motionless in the chair, just as I had left her. I sat back down on the floor in front of her and put my face against her knees. Maybe, close like this, we could both forget what happened.

Mutti was the one who broke the silence.

"I can't take you home with me, my daughter," she said in her softest voice. "I came to tell you something, something important. I'm not well, Lizbeth. You must have heard me cough. I don't know exactly what the matter is, but I'm seeing a doctor. He's good. He's trying some medicine so I can keep working. I should have told you sooner, but I didn't want to worry you."

I could barely breathe. I couldn't move. I just patted my mother's legs and kept my head against them.

"When will you come back, Mutti?" I asked in a whispery voice.

"I don't know. Maybe Thanksgiving. Tante Anna and Onkel Chris have asked me to spend the night with them. We need to talk some things over. I'll have to take the early morning train."

We both stood up and hugged each other.

At the door, Mutti turned to me, her face solemn. "How are you coming along with *Immensee*, Lizbeth?"

I had forgotten all about my beautiful book, *Bee's Lake*.

"I—I haven't had much time, Mutti. The nursery and all."

Mother smiled a little and nodded her head as though she understood. “Just the same, Lizbeth, finish it, please. For me.”

Then she was gone. I went back to the dorm slowly. In a daze, I undressed and took out my beautiful book. Maybe, before lights out, I could read another chapter.

The book seemed to have a halo around it, like an angel—the gold swirls on the cover, the thin tissue covering the pictures. I started to read to myself where I had left off, *Chapter III: In The Forest*: “And so the children lived together; she, often too quiet with him; he, too hearty with her. But they loved being together, just the same . . . ”

That’s as far as I got reading to myself. Evelyn, sitting beside me, studying, put her book down.

“That’s a beautiful book your mother gave you, Lizbeth. How is she, anyway?”

I don’t think I really heard her question. I was still in the story with Reinhardt and Elizabeth.

“She’s—she’s all right—I guess,” I heard myself say.

“Maybe you’d like to read to us from it, Lizbeth,” Evelyn said in her softest voice.

Edna, on the other side joined in. “Yes, Lizbeth. Read out loud. Your mother’s so nice, the book must be nice, too.”

I began to wonder if the girls knew something about my mother that I hadn’t told anybody yet. Maybe they knew more than I did, but maybe, just maybe, reading to them would help us be friends again.

I went back to the beginning of *Bee’s Lake,* translating slowly and soon other girls had gathered round my bed. When I lifted the book to show the picture of Reinhardt carrying Elizabeth out of the forest, I saw Georgiana out of the corner of my eye. She'd propped herself up in bed on her elbow, black curls resting on her hand.

Reading the story, feeling the girls gathered around me, so quiet, listening so carefully, I totally forgot the scene with my mother and the frightening news she told me. I closed the book and put it away in the suitcase under my bed. The last thing I saw before Evelyn turned out the lights was a far-away, sad look on Georgiana's face that I'd never seen before. All I heard in the dark room was the sound of going-to-sleep breathing.

As the days grew shorter and colder, the heaviness in the air at Central got lighter. The boys were back at school, no longer wincing when they moved. Kat had stopped limping and Leland and I were back at work on his math. He was doing well and seemed to have forgotten his beating.

After school I still enjoyed the time in the nursery with Tante Anna and she continued teaching me about baby care and first aide. She said I was a fast learner. I knew my mother would be proud of me. I got cards from her every week and she said she was doing well.

Kat and Georgiana were not as cold and mean to me as they had been, though I knew things between us would never be the same. For one thing, with Georgiana's bed separated from mine, we didn't have that time before going to sleep to giggle and gossip and share secrets. For another thing, Georgiana seemed quieter than she had been, though her temper still flared up like a struck match when she was crossed.

No more tricks were played on me, but the mystery of the red coat stayed a mystery. I began to think about it more as the days got colder. I was sure Georgiana had taken it, but where had she put it?

Almost every night I read aloud to the girls. All of the girls loved the story, I could tell. Georgiana's eyes glittered when I read about Reinhardt's fascination with the gypsy girl. Still, no one said anything, or asked anything about my mother. And I didn't want to talk about it, either. I didn't know why.

A few days before Thanksgiving, we had our first snow. I knew soft flakes were falling, even before I saw them. Everyone else seemed to know, too. We all ran to the windows and watched the snow gently drifting down. It was cozy inside, time to snuggle down in our cots. It was reading time.

I propped myself up with a pillow and reached down under my bed for my suitcase to get out my beautiful book. There, folded neatly on top, was my red coat.

CHAPTER XI

IT WAS SO quiet in the room you could have heard a feather float. It was like the girls all took a breath at the same time and held it. I patted my red coat, shoved it back under the bed like I wasn't surprised, picked up *Bee's Lake*, and started to read.

"*Chapter IV, Christmas Tide.*"

That was as far as I got before all the girls in the dorm let out their breaths and started to giggle. Kat's giggle was higher and louder than all the rest.

"Ain't ya gonna say anything?" Kat squealed.

"You're bansh," I heard Georgiana growl from her corner cot.

"Well, she squealed on us, so I thought—!"

"You're bansh, Kat," Georgiana said. "Think again."

"Lizbeth didn't squeal on you," I heard Evelyn say.

"How'd ya know?" Kat was practically whimpering.

"Miss Schlabaker told me."

"Slopbucket!" Kat spit out. "What does she know?"

"She was there," Evelyn answered, soft and calm.

Evelyn rose to the top of the list of people I loved. I'd miss her when I left Central. And Georgiana! So she wasn't the one who stole my red coat and hid it? Or put flies in my lunch pail and short sheeted my bed?

Nobody said anything more, so I started to read again. I was getting better at translating as I went along, but it was still slow. The girls seemed to know I was doing the best I could.

"Reinhardt and the other students . . . " I translated slowly, jumping to the end of the sentence to find the verb—"met . . . around the oak table . . . in the Ratskeller."

"That's like a Speakeasy today," Georgiana called out.

Where did she get all her information? What a strange, wild girl. I'd never understand her, but I wished I could be more like her. And I wished with all my heart we could be best friends again.

Nothing to do now but read on. "In a corner alcove—sat—a zither girl, with delicate, but gypsy-like features . . . "

I looked over at Georgiana. She had propped her chin on her hand. Her eyes shone. I read on. "Raising his glass to his lips, Reinhardt said, 'I . . . drink . . . to your beautiful, wicked eyes.'"

I heard the girls draw in their breath again. I didn't look up, but went on reading.

"With a scornful laugh she turned to him and said, 'Give me your glass.' Then, fixing her dark eyes full upon him, she drank what was left, and . . . after sounding a chord upon her zither . . . sang . . . in a low, passionate voice:

Look, Love, today,
While yet my face is fair;
Tomorrow, Love,
You will find no beauty there.
One little hour, Love,
All our own;
Then love will be gone,
And I alone . . ."

I couldn't read anymore. I closed the book and put it carefully on top of my red coat. Nobody said anything. Evelyn turned out the lights and the room was dark and quiet. I thought about love—love for my mother, Tante Anna, Evelyn—especially for my wild orphan, Georgiana. I thought about love for the father I couldn't remember. I thought about maybe loving a boy one day the way Elizabeth loved Reinhardt—maybe a boy like Buster? Would I get too old before I found love like that?

It was all so romantic, a round, warm feeling gathered in my heart. Romantic and sad, somehow. I couldn't wait to grow up and learn more about these mysterious things.

I went to sleep wondering—why was my mother so eager for me to finish *Immensee*? What was my father really like? Most of all, I wondered, as I drifted into sleep, what did Georgiana think about all this? And when would I find the chance to talk to her about it?

As it turned out, I didn't have to find the chance. It was Georgiana herself who started talking on our way home from school the very next day.

Ever since their beatings Buster and Clarence kept closer to Leland, and Kat just naturally seemed to tag along with them. It was like a new bond held the three of them together. It was like Kat was mad at *me* for *her* hiding my red coat. Strange.

But Georgiana and I sloshed along together in the melting snow. She started talking like we'd never left off being friends.

"'Member that part in the beginning of *Bee's Lake* where Reinhardt and Elizabeth are children pickin' strawberries in the woods? 'Member how Reinhardt gets all excited about goin' to India n' hitchin' lions to their cart an' drivin' across the desert? An' he wants Elizabeth to follow him an' she says her mother won't let her. An' he says when they grow up no one can order them around, they can do as they please?"

Holy cow, she sure did listen!

"Elizabeth said, 'But my mother will cry.' I remember that part."

"Well," Georgiana took a deep breath. "See, I think that's sort of like you and me. I want to go off and adventure and you wanna to stay home with your ma, doncha think?"

"But I love my mother. I don't want to hurt her."

"See," Georgiana said, kicking slush over my feet. "See what I mean. You're nothin' but a Mama's girl. I betcha in the story Reinhardt goes off and leaves her. Wanna bet?"

I couldn't think of anything to say, so we kept sloshing on, side by side, without another word.

Miss Schlabaker met us at the back door of the Brick House where we always came in.

"There's someone to see you in the parlor, Lizbeth," she announced, smiling like it hurt.

Who would visit me here in Central Orphan's Asylum? I didn't know a single person in the whole town. It was the middle of the week. It couldn't be Mutti, but all the same my heart raced like it was Christmas coming. I forgot Georgiana and rushed down the hall to the parlor.

There stood my mother with her hat and coat still on and her back turned to me. She turned around as I walked into the room. I held out my arms and ran toward her. But instead of her opening her arms to receive me, she held up her hands like a policeman.

"No!" she said. "Don't get too close! Sit down. We must talk!"

Cold fear rippled down my legs. Mutti took off her hat and coat, sat down and pointed to a chair half a room away. Never in my life had my mother acted like this.

Another one of those blurry times comes down like a fog

in my mind. I can't remember the exact order she told me what I needed to know—that she had tuberculosis—that it was very contagious and she mustn't get close to me—that Tante Anna and Onkel Chris had helped her find the doctor who found a place for her in a sanatorium—that she would have to stay there a year or more and that during that time she could only write to me. We couldn't see each other.

I was too numb to understand what she was saying. Mothers didn't get sick. They would always be there. My mother would get over being sick and I'd be back home with her—soon. That was what kept me going here in Central Orphan's Asylum. How could she do this to me?

"Do you understand, Lizbeth?" It was the same dumb question she asked when she first brought me here. My head spun. My mother's face looked fuzzy. I shook my head, made myself look at her steadily to see her more clearly. I noticed she was twisting her handkerchief as she talked and I remember her words as though she spoke them yesterday.

"Lizbeth—before I go—there is more. There is so much I need to tell you—I've been wanting to tell you—before I—before we—"

Mutti stopped, coughed into her handkerchief, started twisting it again, started over, "Lizbeth, if I—while I'm in the sanatorium, you'll be growing up—you'll be starting to become a woman grown—like women do, you know, like I told you—and you need to know—I would like you to know some things—from me—not from anybody else. Oh, not just about menstruation—you know about that—but about me—and—your father."

Now I was fully awake. Present. There, listening. My father, my very own father! My mysterious, lost, beloved father. Now, at long last, I would hear about him.

"Well, you see," she began, "You see, Lizbeth,—we—your father and I—" She stopped, dead still. She straightened her shoulders and blurted out, "We were never married!"

Did I flinch, gasp, blink? I don't know, but Mutti swallowed and hurried on as though time were running out.

"Lizbeth. I have not told you the truth—the whole truth. I didn't think you were ready for it, but now I think you are. You know the book I gave you? *Immensee*? I didn't find it in a book store. Your father gave it to me. We were like Elizabeth and Reinhardt. We loved each other from childhood. But we were so different. Your father was an artist—a painter and a poet. He had a wild and wonderful side, but he had a hard time settling down and my mother was dead set against our ever marrying. Even though I loved your father so much, I didn't want to hurt my mother. She was a widow and not well. My father died when I was a child and she'd struggled for years to make ends meet. That's one of the reasons I took the midwife training, so I could support us—until I fulfilled the dream she had for me by marrying a rich man. So I couldn't—or wouldn't—go away with my beloved Franz and he finally went away without me and got all mixed up with Bohemian artists in the city—they were kind of like gypsies, you see—and—and—he seemed to forget me."

Mutti coughed again, but went right on. She had to get it all out now. I knew her that well.

"And so, while he was gone, I found out I was going to have a baby—you—and the stork didn't bring you, that's for sure. When I told my mother—she was broken-hearted. Then bewildered—then, angry! How could her perfect daughter do this to her? She never forgave me. And within a few months, she got pneumonia and died. She never got to see you. Then I heard through an old friend that Franz had gone to America. Now, you were all I had of love in this world. When I fully realized this, I decided to come to America and start a practice in midwifery and perhaps try and find your father who had a right to know he had a beautiful, beautiful baby daughter."

She stopped suddenly. Then, "So now you know."

No further sound came from my mother, no tears were in her eyes. She held her head high and waited for me, her beautiful daughter to break the silence. But I was her plain daughter, skinny-legged, wispy-haired, homely, really, and I had no thought for the proud, honest mother who sat before her. All I could think of—was me.

"So—I'm a—*bastard*?" I blurted out.

"Don't you ever say that, young lady." Mutti almost shouted. "You were a child of love. And I'll never regret having you. I do regret I was not wiser—and more careful than I was—I regret some of my decisions—but not my *life*."

She sounded finished. But I wasn't. "But—my memories of my father—the woods—picking berries—his holding me on his shoulders—"

Up went Mutti's chin again, reminding me of Georgiana.

"I made those stories up," she went on, "and my stories became your memory. I wanted to capture your father's spirit for you. I didn't have enough courage to follow him so together we could create a life with both freedom and responsibility until too late. I wanted you to know all this before—in case I—"

My mother's voice had faded to a whisper. Her face was a stony mask. Then, she stood up. The last thing I remember of that hour was my mother's words before she left. Through choked sobs she said, "Oh, Lizbeth, you'll never know how much I've loved you—every day of my life—and always will."

CHAPTER XII

YOU CAN'T SAY the children and grown-ups at Central Orphan's Asylum weren't kind. Evelyn hugged me when I walked like into the dorm after my mother left, but I was too numb to return her hug. The grapevine was swift and busy, so everybody seemed to know that my mother had T. B. and was going to a sanatorium—the San, everybody called it.

Kat said, "Holy cow! But she's so nice!" thinking more of my mother than of me, I guess.

Slopbucket came into the dorm, saw me, and said, "That's too bad, Lizbeth."

Georgiana acted like nothing had happened. She just ignored me. For once, I didn't give her a thought. I didn't care.

I couldn't eat any supper, but sat and stared at the fried potatoes and cabbage.

Suppertime, Gashole, came over and put his hand on my shoulder. "*Es tut mir sehr Leid*," he said and I knew it meant 'I'm so sorry' in German.

I was picking at the bread pudding, hard as a rock, when I felt a warm presence behind me and warm hands rubbing my back. Tante Anna, I knew, and when I turned around, I saw her round face and the tall, stately figure of her husband Onkel Chris.

"Come with us, Lizbeth," he said. "We want to talk. You must have some questions, so we'll try to answer them as best we can."

I let them lead me back to the Brick House, to the parlor where I had seen my mother such a short time ago.

"This must come as a shock," Tante Anna began, "even though you knew your mother was not well."

I nodded silently. The girls must have known my mother was sick. Maybe that's why they got nice to me. What would they think if they knew the whole story?

"Tuberculosis is—can be—a very dangerous disease," Onkel Chris went on. "But, fortunately, we've caught it in time. Sunshine, sun lamp treatments, good food, cod-liver oil, and lots and lots of rest will help your mother. The sanatorium will provide all these for her. She'll have the best chance of getting well, right there."

I nodded silently, looking at my feet. I couldn't meet Tante's or Onkel's eyes.

"You'll miss her, we know," Tante Anna said. "But the best thing you can do for your mother is to be as courageous here at Central as she will be in the San."

Another silence. Another nod from me.

"Dear heart," Tante Anna continued, "you mustn't think—you must know in your heart your mother will get well—and that is what will help her get well. She has a wonderful chance of recovering fully—though she'll have to be careful all her life."

I looked up then and saw the two of them leaning in to me. Of course my mother would get well. I couldn't imagine anything else. That was not the problem—it was not seeing Mutti all that time. I needed time alone with her, so we could talk. Learning the truth about my mother and my father—and me—that was the real problem. More than anything in the world I needed to understand the mother I always thought I knew.

I couldn't possibly talk about all this now to Tante and Onkel, so we just sat there. Much as I loved them, Tante Anna and Onkel Chris seemed far away. I really wished they would go and leave me alone.

They finally did, looking worried as they hugged me goodbye.

"We'll be here for you, Lizbeth," Onkel Chris said, and they were gone.

Of course, I didn't read that night. Evelyn was the only one who said anything. "Why don't we change beds, Lizbeth. So you can be next to Georgie. Miss Schlabaker won't know."

I didn't think I cared, but I let her exchange our sheets and got into bed in the old familiar place beside my once-friend.

Soon, the room was quiet. I was grateful when the lights were finally out and the breathing-snoring began. I didn't even try to go to sleep. I just stared into the dark.

After a long time, it seemed, I heard, "Psst," from Georgiana's cot. "Sleep yet?"

All I could manage was, "No."

"I—I shouldn't have said what I did about you bein' a Mama's girl. I—I'm—"

"That's all right."

"No, it ain't."

Silence.

"If your Ma dies you'll be an orphan—like me."

For the first time in hours, I felt fully awake. It was the first time anybody used the word *dies*. I felt as if a huge boulder had dropped right into the room. Mutti might die. I didn't believe it, but everybody else did. My mother, dead. Gone. Maybe in heaven, but that wouldn't do me much good. My ~~had father~~ father had vanished. Now I felt truly, completely an orphan, like Kat, like Buster and Leland and Clarence. Like Georgiana!

I turned toward her. She was lying on her side, head propped on her hand, looking at me.

"What did you say?" I whispered into the dark, as though I hadn't heard her.

"I said, now you might be an orphan like me."

"But I thought you said your mother wasn't dead. I thought you said your mother was a gypsy, and you were going to find her some day."

"I lied. I'm a foundling, Lizzie—a bastard. Slopbucket told me once when she was mad at me. My ma left me on the doorstep of this—this place—with a note. 'No money, no work, no pa. Don't know where the pa is. Take care of her.' "

Two liars in one day, my mother and my best friend. As I lay there, stiff and silent, a strange thing happened. I was feeling closer to Georgiana than I ever had before. Now we were more like sisters. Both orphans. Both bastards with lost fathers.

I reached over for Georgie's hand and squeezed it hard.

"Well, now I can tell you what's really awful. It's not that my mother might die. She won't. She can't! But there is something else—something—"

And the whole story spilled out to my sister-friend, in whispers, in the darkness.

The leaves were gone now and the bare branches of the trees clutched at the sky. The first snow had melted and everything outside looked grey and brown—a dying season. Thanksgiving would soon be here, the time my mother was supposed to have come for a visit.

Things settled back down into their old, familiar routine—walking to school scuffing leaves, helping Leland with his math, walking back to Central with Georgie and stopping off at the Big House to help Tante Anna. The sameness was comforting, in a way. In another, the changeless routine made me feel trapped in Central Orphan's Asylum.

One night, before falling asleep, I looked out the window at the dark autumn sky. I lay under my grey blanket imagining the stars were tiny windows. I imagined those twinkling windows were openings to a wider world that lay beyond the prison I was condemned to. That thought lifted my spirits and helped me fall asleep.

There were some bright spots in the dull days, and for a time they helped me feel lighter. I got to know Onkel Chris better. He came to dinner more often and we'd sing "Ich bin *ein Musikan—*" Miss Schlabaker forgot herself one time and made the best squeaky violin noise you can imagine. Her face got red when we snickered and she didn't do it again.

He taught us a round in German, too, about the *Grosse Uhren* (big clock) going 'tick-tack' and the *kleine Taschenuhren* (little pocket clock) going 'ticky-tacky.' All the orphans singing together sounded wonderful, I thought, but I didn't join in very often.

Father Gastmann stood at the side, his hands behind his back, and never joined in.

Sometimes Onkel taught us some American songs, too. His accent was funny when he sang, "Shkeeters (for skeeters or mosquitoes) am a hummin' on da honeysuckle vine—Schleep (for sleep), Kentucky Pabe (for Babe)." Onkel didn't seem to mind being laughed at. He made it seem more like laughed with than laughed at.

It was good to laugh with all the other orphans, when I felt like it. But it didn't help for long.

On Thanksgiving Day the Ladies Aid from the church in town served us dinner. We had turkey and mashed potatoes (no lumps) gravy, cranberry sauce (which hardly any of us liked), and pumpkin pie (not my favorite). But it was the best meal I'd had since coming to Central.

Before we sat down, Onkel Chris had us all form a giant circle around the dining hall and sing "Be present at our table, Lord" and his deep voice boomed out above all the rest. I joined hands with everybody else, but I still felt outside the circle.

I was glad for the chance to be with Tante Anna in the nursery and I thought for a while I might be able to talk to her. She must have sensed the sadness I couldn't shake, because one afternoon, after the babies had been changed and fed, she pulled the rockers close together and asked me to sit down with her. She didn't take out her crocheting, but turned to me and put her hand on my knee.

"Dear heart," she said. "I know something is troubling you. You must be worried about your mother. It's understandable. But is it something else, something more? If you want to talk about it, I'll surely listen. Sometimes it helps just to talk."

I took Tante's hand and squeezed it tight. I looked at her face, so open, so kind. I longed to let the whole story of my mother's life pour out. I wanted to let her know all about my confusion, my pain. I wanted her comfort. But the words would not come. What filled my mind was a picture of my mother and Tante, sitting together in these same rockers, knitting, crocheting, laughing, sharing thoughts, memories, dreams, as though they had been friends all their lives. It did not seem possible to tell Tante the whole story of my mother's life. Troubled as I was, I could not betray my mother.

"Thank you, Tante," was all I managed to say, "but I'm really all right. I just need time."

"Just as you say," Tante answered. "But remember I am here when you need me."

I stayed a while longer and we talked about the babies, the toddlers, and Christmas coming; and then, I got up, gave her a big hug, and left. It was only Georgiana I could really talk to.

Every night since hearing about Mutti's illness, Evelyn had faithfully changed beds with me after lights were out and Slopbucket hadn't yet found out. That gave Georgie and me the chance to talk. She dreamed up pictures of her dancing gypsy mother, her strong, black-haired father, the Gypsy King. I dreamed up a poet father, both strong and tender. I'd find him somewhere in America and bring him back to my mother and they would marry and we would be a happy family.

We talked about the kind of men we'd marry one day, the kind of life we'd have. I would be a doctor—a doctor who wrote poetry on the side; she would be a gypsy dancer married to the King of the Gypsies and they would dance together in a wild and wonderful way.

"What's a bastard, Georgie," I asked one night. I was pretty sure I knew, but I wanted to know what she thought. She seemed to know so much about gypsies and speakeasies and things I'd never heard of until I met her.

"Don't know for sure. It's when yer Ma and Pa ain't married, like in a church or anything. Seems like if they was a ma and pa they'd be married somehow, doncha think?"

I looked up "bastard" in the big dictionary at school. There was a long list of definitions, like "born out of wedlock" and "illegitimate" and then a long list of other definitions that made me certain it was a terrible thing to be. The word "inferior" came up often in the list. That's the way Gashole spit out the word and Slopbucket, too. That was the way I felt now. How could my mother let me be born inferior?

It snowed the eleventh of December, my mother's birthday. She had been writing every other week and seemed to be getting along well. She liked the San and the people were very kind. I didn't have any money to buy her a present, of course, or a even a card, so I wrote a poem on school paper:

Mother, dear, you're sweeter, far
Than all the other mothers are
Kindness is written on your face
You scatter joy in every place.

It rhymed, but I didn't think it was a real poem. It sounded silly and like something I might have written when I was in kindergarten. I wasn't ready to write about my mother now. Both of us seemed like different persons. But I sent the poem anyway, and Mutti thought it was sweet. I wondered if I ever could be a real poet, like my father. Did my mother have any of his poems? And how could I have memories of my father just from the things my mother told me? I had so many questions about so many things, and no one to give me the answers. Life seemed to get gloomier each day.

After Mutti's birthday, the Christmas Missionary Barrel arrived from one of the churches in another state and was filled with second hand clothes and some candy for all of us. By the time the barrel came to the Brick House, not many clothes were left to choose from, but Slopbucket laid them out on the floor in the parlor and we gathered around and each of us chose something we liked—or needed. Nothing was as beautiful as the mittens Mutti had knitted last fall, except for a sky-blue coat, just my size, just my color.

But I already had a coat—my elegant red one with the hat to match, which had been re-hung in the front closet. I wanted that blue coat with all my heart, but wouldn't let myself reach for it. Kat snatched it up and put it on. It was huge on her. She looked like a little clown, so she took it off and, with a big smile, handed it—to me!

"Here," she said, "just your size and color."

I looked at Georgiana, and she nodded her approval. I tried it on. It was perfect. The girls all clapped. That was the moment I began to feel, just a little, that I belonged. We might be orphans, half-orphans, bastards, inferior—but we were together!

CHAPTER XIII

CHRISTMAS CAME AND we had a perfect snow, just in time. At the Big House a big tree had been put up and everyone helped decorate it with strings of popcorn and cranberries. Tante Anna and Onkel Chris added some delicate ornaments they had brought from Germany—violins, birds, a tiny teapot and a little Santa Claus. On Christmas Eve, everyone from the Brick House went over to the Big House for our Christmas Eve celebration. Onkel and Tante clipped little candle holders to the tree, put small candles in them, and helped the little children carefully light them. Tante and Edna and I brought the babies down from the nursery to see the tree and listen to the singing.

We sang "Up On the Housetop" and "Jolly Old St. Nicholas" and then we opened our presents. The church people had wrapped something for everyone. There were handkerchiefs for the girls, bandanas for the boys, pencils, mittens, socks, even underwear. Each of us received a few coins, which made us feel rich because we never, ever held money in our hands. There were a few pennies for the little children, a nickel for Fourth through Sixth Graders, and a quarter for the older orphans. I gave my nickel to Georgiana for Christmas and she gave me hers. Together we planned to buy and penny candy at the little store on our way home from school—jaw breakers, licorice sticks, coconut flags.

After the present opening, our *Bescherung*, as the Germans called it, Father Gastmann said he had a surprise. We waited. Miss Schlabaker walked to the piano, followed by—Kat! Tiny

Kat, with a fresh bow in her hair sang "When Irish Eyes Are Smilin'" in the sweetest, clearest voice I had ever imagined. It wasn't a Christmas song, but it gave me goosebumps, just the same.

After that Father Gastmann turned out all the lights but the candles. We sang "Silent Night" in English by candle light. Then Onkel Chris sang it in German. Not all Germans were huns, I thought. I didn't believe Georgie thought so either, anymore.

It was all very nice, but still, I was homesick for those cozy Christmases smelling of anise and cinnamon when Mutti and I were together, and I was so innocent about life. What was Christmas like at the San, I wondered. Did my father give her *Immensee* for Christmas when they were together and loved each other so much?

I hadn't read *Immensee* for weeks, but after Christmas, when the early winter darkness locked us indoors right after supper, I began again. With the girls gathered on and around my cot, I began, "*Chapter V—Changes At Home.*" That's the chapter where Reinhardt and Elizabeth start to grow apart and as the days and weeks went by and the reading went on, I knew what the end would be. They would part. Elizabeth would do what her mother wanted and marry the nice man with the brown coat who was steady and rich. Reinhardt would go away and live his gypsy life and forget his true love, Elizabeth. The chapters were getting more and more sad. Why, oh why, didn't my mother go away with my father, why didn't he settle down, marry her, so we could be a real family of three?

I was sick to my stomach when I finished reading each night, but I had to keep on. I had to finish.

Midwinter. The weather as well as Miss Schlabaker locked us in at night and we were locked into the same routine at school and at the asylum. Mutti's letters came less often and from what she wrote, I guessed she felt locked into the Sanatorium, too. It was going to take her months and maybe years to get well. She had to stay in bed much of the time. She sent her love always and asked about Georgiana and Kat and the others. She asked if I had finished *Immensee.*

It was a specially cold night when we read the chapter where Reinhardt gets the letter from his mother saying that Elizabeth had married Erich, the nice, rich, stay-at-home man. The dormitory was cold, so the girls took the blankets from their beds and settled around my bed, making themselves as cozy as best they could.

During the night, we had our first winter thaw and we heard icicles plopping down from the roof. I read about Reinhardt's visit to the beautiful vineyard of Erich and Elizabeth. It was beside the tranquil, dark blue lake, *Immensee,* (I had to look up tranquil in my German dictionary. It means peaceful.) It was spring and the fruit trees were in blossom and there was a "musical hum of innumerable bees (I looked up innumerable, it means many)." Reinhardt had reached his journey's end. The part that made us all cry was the part where the sad and aging Reinhardt has a terrible dream. He dreams he tries to swim out into the lake to get to a water lily and doesn't make it. It lay in the moonlight, just out of his reach.

"That lily is Elizabeth," Evelyn said, wiping her eyes. "He can't reach her. She's too white—too pure!"

"She's bansh," Georgiana hissed through her teeth. "She shoulda gone after Reinhardt. She was nothin' but a Mama's girl—a stay-at home—be nice all the time Mama's girl!"

Georgiana was so loud and fierce, I thought Slopbucket would rush into the room, but she didn't.

I stopped reading and didn't pick the book up again for over a week.

On Valentine's Day, we exchanged cards we'd made at school with red art paper and white paper doilies. We all got a messy one from Buster that said, "Roses are red, violets are blue, when I leave Central, I'll really miss you!"

That's when we found out that Buster had been adopted by one of the trustees and would be leaving Central as soon as school was out. I cried myself to sleep for the first time in months. It seemed like he was Reinhardt and I was Elizabeth and he was leaving me to go off with the gypsies. Georgiana tore up Buster's Valentine and flushed it down the toilet.

Spring came in a sudden burst. Showers washed away the last of the dirtied snow. Leaves unfolded, apple blossoms bloomed over night, daffodils pushed up out of the ground and opened their lovely blossoms. They looked like golden telephones standing in a row in front of the Big House. Tante had planted them last fall, I knew.

School would soon be out and the high school would be holding graduation exercises. Evelyn was going to graduate and leave Central. She'd been accepted at Normal School and would be studying to become a teacher and had been offered a housekeeping job to pay for her room and board.

I felt an emptiness around my heart all the time. I wrote a poem about it:

SPRING
Spring is golden daffodils
and apple blossoms on the hills

Why is my heart so small inside
When it should be opening wide?

I didn't show it to anyone, not even Georgiana.

A few days before graduation, Evelyn asked me to finish *Immensee.* She wanted to know how it ended before she left Central. I knew, but read on. Reinhardt comes to realize he still loves Elizabeth and always will. He guesses she still loves him. She had become so much quieter than she was as a child—so sad. But there was nothing they could do to go back to being innocent children, when they loved each other simply, and walked in the woods together. So he leaves *Immensee*, sadder, but wiser, sure he will never see Elizabeth again in this life.

Then, the story goes back to the beginning with Reinhardt, an old man sitting in the darkness, looking at a small portrait of Elizabeth, touched by moonlight pouring into his room. "Elizabeth," he murmurs softly.

Now, in the story, the old man Reinhardt sees the lake again in his memory and sees the water lily floating all alone on the lake. He can never reach it. There is nothing he can do about the past. He goes back to his writing table and buries himself in his work. The End.

I closed the book carefully and put it under my cot.

The room was quiet for a long time. Then, Evelyn came over and kissed me on the forehead. "Thank you, Lizbeth. I will miss you."

My heavy heart got heavier.

Georgie flopped down on her cot. "I hate it," she spit out. "They shoulda stayed together. They shoulda run away and joined the gypsies!" She pulled the covers over her head and bunched herself up into a little lump. No more talking tonight.

I put the book under my own cot, climbed in and lay on my back, staring at the ceiling. That's when I started dreaming up an idea that might help me understand my father. I had to know why he really left my mother. I had to know more about gypsies. I just had to.

CHAPTER XIV

"WHEN DO the gypsies come through?" I asked Georgie when we were doing our chores that weekend.

"Don't know for sure," she answered without looking up from her furious mopping. "Maybe they're not coming."

"Georgie! They have to come. They have to."

That stopped her and she looked at me, surprised.

"Why?"

We both stopped working and sat on her cot.

"My father may be alive, see! Maybe he joined the gypsies here in America. But even if he didn't, I have to know what they're like. I have to know why he left my mother and lived a gypsy life. What is it about them, Georgie, that's so grand?"

Georgie took a deep breath and let it out in a whoosh. "Well, see, they're—well, they're *free*. They don't have all these rules an' they do what they please when they please an' they dance and sing an' go all over everywhere and don't hafta stay in one place all the time. That's what I like. That's how I know I got gypsy blood."

The longer she talked, the wilder she looked, but she didn't scare me now.

"Well," I said, "why don't we follow the gypsies a little way when they come to town. I can see what gypsies are really like and maybe if you could talk to them you could find out something about your mother!"

Georgie put her hands over her mouth and shook her head in a "no" that made her curls bounce.

"We can't," she said, her voice flat.

"Why, Georgie? Don't you dare?"

Her jaw stuck out and her eyes narrowed. "You didn't get beat up!"

What could I say? I'd hurt her so much. Did I have to get beaten, too, to prove how sorry I was I'd hurt her?

"I'm sorry you got that beating, Georgie, but it won't happen this time. Tante Anna promised us. And the days are longer now. We'll have more time to look and get back before anyone misses us. I just want to see gypsies, Georgie. Just look at them some more. With my own eyes! Please, Georgie!"

She didn't answer. I lifted my chin. "Well then, if you won't go with me, I'll go by myself."

"Dare ya!" she said, and picked up her mop again. "I don't think they're comin' this year, anyway. It's too late."

For once, Georgie was wrong. They came.

It was a grey, cloudy day, hot and muggy. We were playing Chicken Base in the lot behind the Brick House and I got so sweaty and thirsty I wanted to quit, but I didn't want the kids to know. They'd think I was giving up because I couldn't hit the ball very well. I was learning, though. I was trying. Still, it would be wrong to complain and quit.

The gypsies saved me. We heard their music as they rattled into town from the same direction as they'd come last fall. We stopped playing and ran to the street. My heart beat as wildly as the music when I saw the same dancer we'd seen before. She danced so close to us, I thought she might even touch us! Then she gave her tambourine a bang and danced away laughing, like she was teasing. Or daring us to follow?

"They sure are grand," I said, and Georgie looked at me like I was bansh.

The gypsies had come so suddenly I didn't have time to think or plan. I had no idea how we were going to get away from the other kids and follow them. We'd have to do something soon, or the gypsies would disappear before we could catch up with them, and it would be like last fall.

A low rumble of thunder and a few fat plops of rain helped. I saw that I wasn't the only one limp from the heat. Half of us stopped playing, looked up at the sky, and held out our hands to feel the cool rain drops. The boys picked up the bat and balls and we all ran for the Brick House.

It was the perfect time. I said I wanted to wash up and Georgie followed me, but we didn't go to the girls' room. Without a word to each other, as though we had planned it all out, we went down the hall to the parlor and out the front door. I prayed Slopbucket wouldn't see us.

We didn't pay any attention to the light rain and started across the corn field. How we got away without being seen, I don't know. I had an idea the gypsies followed the road out of town and then went into the woods to camp by the river, like Georgie said. We headed for the woods.

At the edge of the woods, we looked back to see if anyone had followed us. Nothing but young cornstalks poked up, row after row, stiff and still. The trees ahead of us seemed much closer together than they had last fall. Shrubs and vines underneath them looked like a dark green wall we'd never get through.

I pushed through the bushes in the best opening I could find, Georgie still following me. Twigs and stickers scratched my arms and legs. It was hotter and stickier here inside the woods than it had been in the open, but at least the trees and bushes would hide us from anyone following us. Once in a while, we heard low thunder, but still I stumbled on, acting like I knew what I was doing.

I heard Georgie puffing behind me. "Boys sure is lucky, wearing pants. Wish I had on a pair of overalls to cover my legs."

"Or those knickers you see in magazines. Women's knickers."

That's all the talk we had breath for.

The woods were getting deeper and darker and I wondered which direction to go in. I began to think maybe this was a crazy idea, but I pushed the thought away. This time, I was not going to be the scaredy cat. This time, I was in the lead. I would find the way. The river where we'd find the gypsies had to be somewhere. The woods couldn't go on forever.

It was still early afternoon, I thought. It had to be. So why was it getting darker so fast?

I stopped and looked up, trying to see the sky through the tree tops towering over us. Big, dark clouds frowned down at us, rolling over us, shutting out the light, growling with thunder. The rumbles grew louder, the clouds lower. A summer storm. I should have known one was coming. I hadn't been thinking.

A crack of lightening hit the forest, lighting it, turning it a sick green. I looked at Georgie and reached for her hand just as the wind picked up and twisted our dresses round our legs. The trees swirled, whipping back and forth above us. I felt like we were being punished for running away, not letting anyone know where we were going. Never had I seen a storm like this, much less been out in it.

Where to go? Which direction to run? Which way was home, the orphan's asylum? In that moment, for the first time, that's the way I thought of Central. I looked around me and in every direction the forest looked the same. There was nothing but trees and underbrush, walls of ugly green. I couldn't move at all. I was lost! We were lost. I'd gotten us lost.

The thunder got louder by the second and the lightening closer. A huge bolt of thunder and lightening struck at the same moment. Georgie tightened her grip on my hand and together we stumbled toward the nearest tree. Just then the rain began to gush down on us like a waterfall. We were soaked in minutes. I was beginning to feel cold—after being so hot.

"Which way's out?" asked Georgie, through chattering teeth.

"I—I don't know for sure." I tried to keep the whimper out of my voice. "What do you think?"

"I don't know neither."

We just sat down right where we were, leaned our backs against a tree trunk, and let the rain pour down. There was nothing else we could do.

The thunder and lightening stopped as suddenly as it had come. But the rain came on down, steady, heavy. We were soaked to the skin in seconds.

I hated asking Georgie what to do, I felt like such a failure, but I couldn't help myself. I was shaking all over.

"What shall we do, Georgie?"

"Guess we have to find our way back. Gashole will be so mad, he'll kill us—or me, anyway—if we don't get back before dark."

My bottom prickled with a different kind of fear. Father Gastmann, mad at Georgie again—and *me* this time? Tante Anna did promise to protect us, but running away without telling anybody and getting lost? Even Tante Anna couldn't save us from punishment. I could almost feel the blood running down my legs.

"Let's go, Georgie." I said. "Let's keep trying to get out of here, and getting home before dark.

"Okey-dokey, Lizzie. Let's go."

Georgie hadn't complained a single bit and she wasn't blaming me for anything. I had to get her out of here and back to Central, even if I bled to death from Father Gastmann's whipping.

So we sloshed our way through the underbrush, the rain still falling in buckets. I'd read somewhere that you could tell north from the moss on the trees, but I couldn't find any moss and I didn't know if Central was North, South, East, or West. We seemed to be going around in circles.

"We have to stop. Georgie," I said. "If we keep on, we'll only get more lost. Maybe the rain will stop pretty soon. If the sun comes out, maybe I can tell which way to go." I was trying to sound like a leader again, even if I didn't feel like one.

"Or maybe, you-know-who, from you-know-where will find us and drag us home and we'll get beat up. Or I will—if he doesn't kill me first," Georgie answered.

I didn't try to argue. I was too tired. I'd prove my courage later. "I think the rain is letting up," I said.

It was letting up. And then it stopped, as suddenly as it began.

We both looked at the sky, and saw the clouds breaking up and the sun doing its best to shine through. I could have shouted with joy.

But I was too tired to shout and secretly prayed that rescuers from Central would be searching for us. I prayed that they would find us soon, even if it meant beatings and weeks of going to bed without supper.

"Maybe we should just stay in one place and start yelling, so if anybody is looking they can find us easier," Georgie said.

Now that the rain had stopped, swarms of gnats and mosquitoes buzzed around us. We swatted and scratched and tried to brush the pests away from our ears. I looked at my friend. Blood was oozing down her neck and arms from the pesky bugs that were biting us. She didn't look so wild and wonderful now. Her black, shiny curls were matted and stuck together with clumps of dirt and twigs and leaves.

"Oh, Georgie," I said, "how did I ever get us in this mess? It was such a dumb idea. You won't get punished without me, this time, I promise."

Georgie looked at me without smiling—or frowning, either. Did she believe me? I couldn't tell. Then she lifted her nose up in the air like little dog and started sniffing.

"Guess what," she said. "I smell smoke."

I started sniffing, too, smelled the smoke, and heard dogs barking in the distance, maybe from some farm and the farmers could rescue us. But what if the lightening had started a forest fire and the dogs were barking a warning. Were we trapped? A thunder storm and getting lost was bad enough—but, now, a fire?

I forgot about getting soaked, being lost, getting punished. All I could think about was finding where the fire was!.

"Guess what! I think it's somebody's campfire," Georgie said. "I'm hungry and thirsty. And I have to pee!"

CHAPTER XV

We didn't have to look far to find lots of places for relieving ourselves. The woods were far more private than the toilets in the Girl's Room at Central. Not that it mattered now, after everything we'd been through. Just the same, I looked for a place and I couldn't believe what I saw. Sloshing around in the driving rain, we had somehow found our way to a clearing. We were at the edge of the forest. The sun shone so brightly you'd never know there'd been a storm. Birds sang, fluttering and flying above us. Then, louder than the bird calls, I thought I heard the sound of rushing water.

"The river!" Georgie squealed. She'd heard it, too. "We found our way to the river. I can get a drink of water!"

"And we'll be safe from fire there. We can stay there at the river's edge and start our yelling. We'll be easy for some farmer to find us there. Come on, let's go!"

We ran toward the sound and discovered we were at the top of a cliff. There were no trees and not one bush. Nothing but sandy soil and rocks covered the bank. Far down below us, we saw the river, sunlight flickering in little dots on the water. We could have slipped and fallen far down in all that dark and rain. it reminded me of the place we had been in last fall. Way back then I'd been afraid I'd get dirty or hurt sliding down the bank. Now, I didn't wait a second. I slid on my bottom, just behind Georgie, to the very edge of the water. Laughing and shouting, we knelt on the bank and plunged our hands into the river, splashing it over our dirty, mosquito-bitten faces. We didn't give the fire a second thought. We cupped our hands and filled them with water and were lifting them to our mouths and starting to drink when we heard an awful shriek upriver from us. We froze. Was it animal or human? We looked in the direction of the scary sound.

There, not a room's length away, was a kind of person I had never in my life seen before, an old, old woman with a long, dark skirt and a bright red and yellow kerchief round her head. She was pointing one bony finger at us and shrieking something in a language we couldn't understand. "Ga—Ga—Gee—Gee."

With the other hand she made a motion that seemed to mean—"Go away!" Was she saying, "Get out of here?"

A witch, I thought, though I didn't believe in witches. Maybe she wasn't real. Maybe my fear was making me see a vision. I felt like I was under a spell and couldn't move or talk.

Georgie broke the spell. "It's a gypsy!" she breathed. "We found 'em!"

I was still scared to death, though, and I couldn't believe it when I saw Georgie put her hand out like someone trying to tame a wild animal and walk slowly toward the old woman.

"I'm a gypsy, too!" she called.

The dark figure yelled on, like she hadn't heard Georgie. The closer Georgie got, the louder the old woman screamed shouting, "Gadje! Gadje! Go! Go!"

Georgie kept moving toward her, hand still out. I was frozen to my spot.

Then the old gypsy started moving toward us, picking up a stick and lifting it like she was going to hit Georgie. She was close enough now for me to see her leathery skin and her eyes. They narrowed and glared with hatred, reminding me in a flash of Georgie's first look at me.

Georgie held her ground and the old woman was about to swing her stick to strike at her when I heard a loud, clear voice call out in the same strange language. The gypsy–witch slowly lowered her stick and stopped shrieking.

We looked past the old woman, trying to see where the call was coming from.

Moving toward us in long, graceful strides, flowing skirt swaying, earrings jangling, was the dancer with the flashing smile and dazzling teeth.

Behind her ran a gang of raggedy looking children screeching like wild animals. They picked up stones and started throwing them at us, yelling at the top of their voices. When they were close enough to hit us, Dancer turned and swatted one of the boys on his bottom. He dropped his stone, stood stock still and started to laugh. My mouth dropped open. In my world didn't laugh when their bottoms were swatted. These children weren't afraid. They crowded around Dancer and the old witch who were standing, nose to nose, waggling their fingers and shouting at each other.

Old witch finally calmed down walked away and the children straggled after her. They looked back at us, shouted, laughed, and disappeared into the woods. Dancer watched them leave, then slowly walked up to us, her jewelry clinking and glistening in the morning sun.

"You run away?" she asked with her shiny smile.

I backed away from Dancer.

"Well, we—" I stammered.

Georgie stood her ground, stuck her chin out. "I'm lookin' for my ma."

"In gypsy camp?" Dancer asked, raising her black eyebrows.

"Yup! My ma's a gypsy."

"How you know?"

"I just know. Ma left me—on—on—somebody's doorstep—when I was a baby."

Dancer threw her head back and laughed so loud it made an echo in the river valley.

"Ha! You no gypsy! No gypsy woman leave child. Why? We all take care of. Whole tribe. Whole kumpania. Unless—" She suddenly got serious and peered into Georgie's eyes. "Unless she take up with Gadje man. Gadje white. Very, very bad. Against law. Gypsy law."

Gadje, kumpania—strange words. What did they mean? Georgie lowered her chin and stared back at Dancer, whose mood changed again, fast as lightening.

"Ha!" she said and flashed her bright smile at me. "You no gypsy, for true. You Gadje, light hair, blue eye. But you both wet. Come."

She put her arm around Georgie, gestured to me and we let ourselves be led back into the woods, away from the river, farther away from Central, I guessed.

"My name La Lubja," she said as we walked along beside her. "I dance for Gadje in winter. Come back, in summer, to families, our kumpania. La Lubja tell fortunes—fairs—circuses. I learn English. Learn read, write. Learn Gadje ways. I know you from orphan place. I know you run away. I see much things, know much things. Gadje have orphans—no gypsy, no Rom have orphans. No such thing. Mother, father die, kumpania take in."

La Lubja stopped and looked at us again. Her dark eyes gleamed as she searched our faces, first Georgiana's, then mine, back and forth. Those eyes seemed to look way in to us, like she was trying to figure us out. My eyes felt bluer than they ever had in my life, my hair thinner and paler, my skin whiter.

The gypsy dancer threw her head back again and laughed. "You run away, yes? Well, we take you back. Gypsies not steal children. Only Gadje think so. Enough trouble with Gadje. But first, we dry you. First, we feed you."

"You," she said and ran her fingers through Georgie's hair. "You think you gypsy—Rom? Ha! We see," and her skirts swirled around her legs as she moved toward the woods.

Georgie and I followed her like lost lambs. She was the most graceful person I'd ever seen in my life. So strong, too. A grown-up Georgiana, maybe? Would my father have—? Is this the kind of person my father would have—? I pushed the thought out of my mind as we let La Lubja lead us through the underbrush.

CHAPTER XVI

As La Lubja led us through the thicket, the smoky smell got stronger. Blue smoke spirals rose above the tree tops. The dogs' barking got louder and voices, some high and clear, some deep and strong, filled the air.

The brush we had been pushing through stopped and we were at the edge of a huge clearing. How had the gypsies found it in the middle of the forest?

Spread out in front of us on shrubs around the clearing was a flower garden of quilts and blankets, drying in the sun, red and yellow, green and blue, and behind that was a half circle of wagons and horses. Scattered here and there were small fires with women bending over them cooking. Children tumbled around with each other and the raggedy dogs. The men hung around the wagons and horses, smoking, laughing.

La Lubja led us to the nearest fire. Shouting children and barking dogs gathered around us. No stone throwing this time. One of the boys pointed to our bare, scratched legs, covered his eyes with his hands, turned and ran. La Lubja pushed us down near the fire and covered our legs with a bright quilt.

"Marimé," she said, "Bare legs is curse with Rom. Is Gypsy law. You young. No matter. But we find you long skirt before we take you back."

Across the fire from us sat a hunched up figure with a red and yellow kerchief twisted around her head—the gypsy witch who had raised her stick at us. She was quiet, but glared at us still. La Lubja noticed.

"That Shika, old wise one. She best fortune-teller. She know all. See all. She know Gadje our enemy. You Gadje. You break gypsy law when you drink from river at wrong place. Drink upstream first, then wash place, then horse place. You drink horse place. She protect you when she chase you away. She not evil. But, she know Gadje bring curse to Rom. They chase, we run. Hide."

I had a lot of questions, but I didn't dare ask any. I just looked all around at these strange, wild people and pulled the quilt up to my chin. Georgie was squirming beside me. All of a sudden, she jumped up, pulling the cover from me and wrapping it around her waist.

"I'm a gypsy!" she shouted, "I know it! I'm no Gadje! See my hair, my eyes. See me dance!"

She knotted the quilt tight around her waist and started to move her arms and fingers and swing her hips just as she had that night I found her in my red coat, dancing in the moonlight.

A twirl or two and La Lubja joined her, guiding her. The other women formed a circle round them and started clapping and laughing and shouting. I sat scrunched up in my quilt.

The dogs started barking louder and the men began strolling over toward us. The man in the lead was huge. All wore hats but his was the biggest of all and had a bright yellow band around it. He wore it at an angle, pulled over one eye. He had a big belly, a big moustache and wore an earring! In spite of the moustache, he didn't look at all like Father Gastmann. None of the men looked anything like I dreamed my father would look either. The big man wore his stomach in front like he was proud of it and started clapping a rhythm for Georgie's dancing.

The closer he came to us, the more the women, children and other men drew back, making a circle around La Lubja and Georgie. He motioned to some younger men behind him who had instruments hanging from their shoulders—a guitar, a violin, a tambourine. Everybody who didn't have an instrument clapped. Everybody shouted.

Georgie danced with La Lubja as though she had taken lessons all her life. Before long, other gypsies joined them. It was like a party, a wild and wonderful party in the middle of the day. I tried to imagine my poet father dancing with them. I couldn't. Mutti? Unthinkable. And the thought of Gashole and Slopbucket dancing like this—impossible!

Wildly as they danced, none of the women showed their legs. *Marimé*. I remembered the word. Since Georgie had taken the quilt, I sat with mine tucked under me, hiding them as best I could. I didn't want to curse anybody. I wouldn't have dared to try to dance, even if I had a long skirt. I didn't even clap.

Watching them, I began to feel lonely again. I wondered what was happening at the orphans' asylum and hoped they would be out looking for us. I thought about Kat and Leland and Evelyn and Tante Anna. I could see Georgie was having a wonderful time with what might really be her family. In a way I was happy for her but I really wished the dancing would stop and Georgie would come back and sit next to me and cover my legs with the quilt so I could stretch them out. I was hungry, too. A big sap sandwich would taste wonderful right now.

Everyone was making so much noise, clapping and shouting, that only the dogs noticed another commotion. The underbrush at the edge of the clearing parted. The dogs snarled, the dancing stopped. The men rushed to the horses and wagons, the women scurried to gather the scattered quilts and put out the fires. Only the big man stood firm, legs apart, facing the uniforms and clubs and mean faces of the policemen before him.

"Where are the children, you child stealers?" the tallest policeman growled.

I held my breath. I thought of Georgie's sudden anger when she was crossed and worried a fight would break out. But the big man just stood and looked the policeman in the eye!

"Ha!" he said, calmly. "Who would steal useless children? Here, you take." He grabbed Georgie by the shoulder and pushed her at the policeman.

"No! No!" Georgie shouted. She broke away from the policeman's grasp, flew to La Lubja and threw her arms around her.

La Lubja gently, but firmly, loosened Georgie's grasp, placed her hand on her hip and swayed toward the policeman, lowering her eyes and smiling at him in a knowing kind of way. She stepped in front of him, and with a great sweep, lifted her skirts, showing her legs all the way up to her hips.

The gypsies went about their business as though nothing had happened. *Marimé.* La Lubja had put a curse on the policeman. He just looked at her and winked in a secret way. He didn't know anything about gypsy curses.

"Gypsy no steal children," La Lubja said sweetly. "But we keep run-away? No? We adopt? Yes?"

She turned to the big man. "Putja, we keep children, no?"

"No!" Putja answered in English. Then he spoke rapidly in the strange language and La Lubja raised her arms like she was saying, "Well, I tried," and went back to stand beside Georgie.

The big man, Putja, came over to me, pulled me up from the ground, placed my arm on his and led me to the policeman, like I was a princess,

"Here. Here is Gadje child. She thin. She useless. You take."

Then he walked slowly over to Georgie, pulling her from La Lubja's side and walked her over to the policeman.

"Here. Here is gypsy child. You steal from us." He turned then, and in a most dignified way took his time walking back to the men and horses.

"Dirty gypsies," the policeman growled, "get out of here. Move! Be gone by nightfall—or else!" He grabbed Georgie by the arm to lead her away.

"No!" Georgie screamed.

I heard a yelp from the policeman and saw Georgie's head bent over his arm. She'd bitten him!

"I'm not going!" Georgie yelled. "I'm a gypsy, I tell ya! I belong!"

"Dirty little gypsy," the policeman ground out between his teeth. "You're coming whether you like it or not!"

He swatted Georgie's across the face, twisted her arms behind her back and marched her through the bushes. I wanted to run after her and pound my fists against the policeman's back, but another policeman took one of my hands in his own, put his other firmly on my shoulder and I let myself be led.

Ahead of me I heard Georgie's screams turn to deep, heartbroken wails. I thought my heart would break along with hers. I wanted her to be happy, yes. I understood her longing to be with people more like her than anyone else she had ever known. But more than anything in the world, I wanted her to stay with me, my first real friend. My insides felt like they were pulling apart.

Behind me, the dogs were still barking, the horses snorting. The wagons creaked and groaned as they were being moved. I heard no gypsy voices. I turned back to see them one more time. They were piling the wagons with all their goods, getting ready to leave. La Lubja saw me, waved her hand at me, then turned and strolled away. That's the last I saw of her.

CHAPTER XVII

THE POLICEMEN hung on to us and led us back through the underbrush until we came to a road where a police car was parked. One of them put me in the front seat and the other hung on to Georgie as they crawled in back. I looked at Georgie before I got in. She wasn't crying so hard anymore but sat with her arms crossed against her chest, scowling.

It was very quiet as we bumped along the gravel road and it seemed a long way back in to town. We parked in front of the police station and still, no one spoke a word.

I wanted to run to Georgie and put my arms around her to comfort her, but the policeman held on to her with a tight grip. We were marched up the steps and into an office where the police chief stood, and beside him—Father Gastmann.

This was so much worse than my first day at Central. Then, I had been a little girl, afraid of things I couldn't imagine. Now, the fear was real. Now, I was afraid that we'd be beaten, no matter what Tante Anna said. We'd have to go without supper—for how long? And mother would find out and be heartbroken. They might even send us to juvenile prison.

"Here they are, Father Gastmann. We found them in the gypsy camp, wet and frightened. Dirty gypsies claimed they didn't steal them. But I sent them packing, anyway."

Silence. The policeman looked at the chief, the chief looked at Father Gastmann, Father Gastmann looked at me, his expression never changing.

"Well, Father Gastmann," the chief of police said, "It's up to you. We were only ordered to find the children. Do you want to press charges, or not? I know Putja, and he's a sly old fellow. His band's pretty good, but they're thieves, for sure. We've been told they steal children. They'll have slipped away if we don't follow them soon.

I held my breath as I looked at Father Gastmann. What would he say? Would he blame the gypsies, like everybody else?

"*Ja,*" he said, "this must stop—this child stealing—this thieving. Who knows what's next."

I looked over at Georgie for help. The scowl was gone. Her head had dropped and she looked helpless for the first time since I'd known her. The fire that was so much a part of her had gone out. It was up to me now. Oh God in Heaven Above, make me brave, I prayed silently.

I heard a voice and knew it was mine, though it didn't seem to belong to me. I had no idea what was going to come out of my mouth.

"No!" the voice said, strong, definite. "The gypsies didn't steal us. They didn't. They found us after the storm. They took us in. They were nice. They were going to bring us back. They were."

Father Gastmann looked at me for a long time with wide eyes. Then his eyes narrowed and he looked at Georgie, whose head was still hanging.

"No," he said to the police chief, "I think this is an Asylum matter. We'll take care of it at Central, first. Then we'll see."

With that, he put one hand on the back of my neck and the other on Georgie's and walked us firmly out the door.

We rode home—to Central, I mean—in the police car. We were marched into the Big House, shoved into the dark space under the stairs where we waited for Father Gastmann to call us into his office.

I was the first to be called. He would see us one at a time and compare our stories, I guessed.

"Well, Miss Lizbeth," he said, after pacing in front of me for hours, it seemed, scowling all the while. "What have you to say for yourself? After all we've done for you here at Central. Special privilege, working with Tante Anna, letting your mother stay here weekends. Seems you tagged along after Georgiana, after all. Let her influence you, lead you astray. I must say, I'm disappointed. Your poor mother."

I pictured Georgie, huddled under the stairs, waiting for the beating, wet, hungry, very, very sad. It was not my mother I thought of now—but my friend, Georgiana.

I lifted my chin. My heart was beating. "Father Gastmann, it wasn't Georgiana's idea to follow the gypsies. We didn't plan to run away. We got lost. I got us lost. It wasn't Georgie's fault. It was mine."

"Miss Lizbeth" Father Gastmann was mad enough that his voice got louder. "You know Georgiana—she's—she's a wild one."

Without warning, anger busted open inside me, for the second time in my life.

"Father Gastmann, stop blaming Georgiana for everything," I practically shouted.

Father Gastmann banged his fist on his desk. "How dare you talk back to me, young lady."

I wasn't Mama's girl anymore. I was a tiger, defending my mate. I felt huge, hot, strong. I shouted louder. "Somebody has to. Everybody's afraid of you. Don't you know that! Everything's not Georgie's fault. What have you got against her? She's special. She's brave and free and—and—just wonderful."

I had started to cry now. I didn't know what was coming.

But I couldn't stop blubbering, "She's my best friend. I wish I was more like her. It's my fault. All of it. I wanted to find the gypsies. She didn't want to. She didn't. If you have to beat somebody, beat me, Father Gastmann. Beat me!" I crumpled to the floor, sobbing.

Father Gastmann didn't say one word. After a long, long time, I heard his voice coming from far away. "We'll see, Miss Lizbeth. Get up off the floor. Right now! Send Georgiana in."

I got to my feet somehow and walked out the door, without looking at Father Gastmann.

I walked to the closet under the stairs, and peered into the dark cave, whispering, "Georgie?" I got no answer. I pushed and shoved the mops and brooms and boots and shoes out of my way. Nothing warm and human was there. Georgie was gone.

CHAPTER XVIII

"WHERE'S GEORGIE?" I asked the girls in the dorm. I was out of breath. I had searched the wash room in the Big House, run down the walk to the Brick House, searched the washroom there, looked under Georgie's bed, into the parlor and back to the dorm.

"Where is she?" I demanded.

"Where've ya been?" they all asked at once.

"Where is she? Where'd she go?"

It was Evelyn who finally answered. "She ran in, Lizbeth. Then she ran out. She must be outside in the sand lot with the boys. Where were you two?"

"What happened?" Kat squeaked.

"Tante Anna's worried," Edna whined.

I ignored them all. No time. I ran outside to the sand lot, where the boys were playing ball.

"Where's Georgie?" I grabbed Clarence's bat right out of his hands. "Did you see her?"

"You're bansh, Lizzie? She ain't here. We ain't seen her. Where were you? Didja run off or what?"

"Didja get beat up?" Leland cried out.

No time. I ran back to the Big House fast as I could go and up the stairs to the nursery. Tante Anna would know what to do. I couldn't face Father Gastmann again.

"Where's Georgie? Did you see her, Tante?"

Tante Anna came over to me in two steps and took me in her arms. "My child, where were you? What happened?"

I wanted to stay right there in those sheltering arms, but I couldn't. There was no time to lose.

"Oh, Tante, Georgie's run away—to join the gypsies. And she may never find them. And it's my fault, it's all my fault. We've got to find her and bring her back before something happens to her. They'll disappear and we'll never know if she found them. We'll never find Georgie. We just have to know where she is."

I broke down again and let myself be patted by Tante Anna.

"Not so fast, Lizbeth. Not so fast. Start from the beginning. Tell me what happened."

Because she was the one grown-up around that I trusted, I started at the beginning and told her everything—all about my mother and father—about my wanting to see how the gypsies lived, wanting to understand my father, maybe even find him. I told her about the storm, about our time with La Lubja and Putja's band, and even my yelling at Father Gastmann.

It was good to tell it all to someone—someone who just listened, which she did. And she didn't say one word or ask one question until I had finished.

"Well, dear heart, I know this is hard but we must tell Father Gastmann. I'll call Oncle Chris first. We'll both go with you. We must try to find Georgiana soon—if we can. But first. Have you eaten? And what about changing your dress? You'll feel better."

Tante stayed with me the entire time while I washed and changed clothes. Then, she took me into the kitchen for bread and cold sausage and while I swallowed a few bites, she called Onkel Chris and told him the story.

All three of us went to see Father Gastmann. With Tante and Onkel beside me, I could talk without crying. With them beside me, I knew Father Gastmann would put his best foot forward. He would put his attention on finding Georgie instead of on me. They decided the place to start asking the police to try and find Putja's band.

Father Gastmann picked up the telephone.

I clenched my fists, wanting to stamp my feet and yell, "Don't call the police, please! Why aren't we getting on with it? All this talk is taking time, time away from finding Georgie."

But I held myself back. With Tante and Onkel there, I just couldn't yell. My ears rang. My head felt so heavy I couldn't hold it up. I clenched my teeth to keep the tears back.

The police came to the Brick House and I had to tell them everything we'd learned from La Lubja, that gypsy bands gather summers in groups, like families, that they called them kumpanias, that moved around a lot—fairs, circuses.

I rambled on and on, choked with fear. They could easily hide her, I told them. They'd be afraid Central would take her back and she wouldn't want to go. I knew how she felt but I was so afraid for her. She might get really lost looking for Putja's band, or have a terrible accident and—and—my mind stopped working. I couldn't even think the word.

The police thanked me, and left. The search was on.

All during the summer days and weeks that followed, my heart was heavy. I didn't cry at night, but had a hard time going to sleep. I tossed and turned, thinking about Georgie, wondering if she'd found the gypsies. Was her mother really a gypsy? Would she ever find her? And her father? Was he a Gadje? And how would the gypsies treat her if she was. Would she be an outcast? And if she didn't find Putja's band would she be truly lost? Would she get dirtier, hungrier, wilder, lonelier every day? Would she maybe start to miss me and be sorry she had run away.

It was all my fault. I worried so much about her that I forgot everything else—the story of my birth, Mutti's being in the San, finding my father. I missed Georgie so much. My misery had no end.

Tante Anna let me know how the search was going. She took the time every day in the nursery, pulled our rockers close and filled me in. From her I learned that the local police were still looking, but had found no trace—no Georgiana, no La Lubja, no Putja's band.

One day she took my hand as she told me the latest news, "The state police have been asked to seek out gypsies at every county fair in the state. They've been scouring the countryside and examining accident reports to see if Georgie had been in one of them. So far they've found no trace of Georgiana. But, dear heart, we won't give up."

The leaves were turning color when school began again. It had been a year since I first came to Central. I was in the seventh grade now but there wasn't much difference because the same teachers taught junior high as taught the younger kids, and we were all in the same building, first grade through high school. I still worked with Leland but not as much as the year before. I missed Evelyn and Buster but not nearly as much as I missed Georgie. I got cards from Mutti regularly. She was getting better but not even that joy stopped my hurting.

At the end of the first week of school, when I walked in to the nursery, Onkel Chris was there.

"Lizbeth," he said "We have good news!"

But his face didn't look like good news. He took both my hands in his huge ones and led me to one of the rockers.

"We've found Georgiana!"

I started up out of my chair. Onkel Chris guided me back down.

"Now this is the part that is hard, Lizbeth. Several days ago Father Gastmann got a letter from a lawyer representing Putja. A few non-gypsy lawyers do work in behalf of gypsies. Somehow, by some miracle, Georgiana did find Putja and his band and he applied for the adoption of Georgiana. She wants to stay with the gypsies."

"But . . . she can't! We can't let her!"

"We may not have a legal claim on her," Onkel continued. "She was left in our care with a note from her mother. Seems her mother's wish was for us to care for her, but that note, sad to say, has been lost. We would have to go to court for custody. That would be hard and long."

All the air I'd been holding in came out in a whoosh. I went to the door, turning my back to Tante and Onkel. Part of me, I knew, I was not being grateful, but I couldn't help myself. I couldn't seem to be happy for Georgiana, if it meant unhappiness for me.

"It's all my fault," was all I could say.

"No, Lizbeth," Onkel Chris said firmly. "Please turn around and look at me. That's taking too much responsibility. Georgiana has a mind of her own. Maybe this is best for her, after all. We may have to let her go."

I turned around. "Never! Georgiana belongs here—with me!"

Tante and Onkel said nothing and I walked out the door without thanking them.

That night I lay awake, staring at the empty cot beside me.

I wanted to reach out and touch it although that would only make the emptiness more real. I wished I could cry but the heavy feeling inside me was too deep for tears. The heaviness had hold of me and I didn't have the strength to push it away. I was glad my mother was better. I was glad Georgie was safe and living with people she wanted to be with. But didn't she miss me? Why didn't she let me know, somehow, she was all right. And why did she want to stay with the gypsies? They had rules, too, just different ones from ours. How free were they, really, running from the police, always on the go? Would the gypsies always be kind to her? Would it always be the wonderful world she felt she belonged in?

That night I lay on my cot listening to the heavy breathing and the snores of my orphan sisters. When I felt sure everyone was asleep, I got up out of bed.

Autumn moonlight shone through the small window above my cot. It reminded me of that night so long ago when I found Georgie dancing in the parlor wearing my red coat.

My red coat! I needed to see it now, to feel its warmth around me. It was more than something to wear. It was my tie to the mother who had made it for me so long ago. It reminded me of elegance. Most of all, it might bring me close to Georgie.

The night light was on in the hall and the parlor door open. I tip-toed to the closet. This time, my red coat was there. I took it down and put it on, slipping my arms into the sleeves and pressing the soft squirrel collar against my cheek. I put my hands into the pockets seeking warmth and started to sway back and forth, beginning a dance, a gypsy dance.

The pockets were deep and inside the right one my cold fingers touched something that rattled. A crumpled piece of paper! I hurried to the chair and the lamp beside it, turned it on and uncrumpled the paper, forgetting I might wake Slopbucket.

There it was, my message from Georgie, her last words to me:

> Dear Liz,
>
> I hope you find this note sometime. I wanted to say good-bye but I didnt have time. Im going. Understand please I have to find the gypsies. my ma maybe. you came to Central I didn't like you. You had a ma I didn't. You had a red coat. The grown-ups liked you. You belong I dont belong. Now I like you I love you like roses are red violets are blue and I will never forget you and some day I will be good like you a little. Sometimes I think I already am a little. Do you understand your pa better? Hope you find him someday If I get a chance, I'll ~~rig~~ write. Let me go, now liz.
>
> Your Best ~~Fiend~~ Friend Georgie, the gipsee.

I smoothed the paper, turned out the light, went back to my cot. Before I crept in, I went to Georgie's cot and stroked the covers, over and over. I took her note and placed it carefully between the pages of *Immensee*, right next to the picture of Reinhardt's gypsy.

CHAPTER XIX

GREY DAYS FOLLOWED. For weeks, everything was wrapped in grey. I got up to a grey sky, washed, ate grey lumpy oatmeal, went to school, climbed the stairs in the Big House to help Tante Anna. No babies lay in the cribs any more. They'd all grown up and out of their cribs, and were crawling and wobbling across the floor. After work every day, I ate supper, got ready for bed, wrote in my diary and sometimes read, but not out loud to the other girls.

One diary entry, November 19, 1928:

> Dear Diary:
>
> Last night I dreamed I was on a railroad track and a train was coming and I couldn't move my legs. It was terrible, but I didn't cry out. I still miss Georgie like the dickens. I can't talk to anybody, even Tante Anna, like I could talk to Georgie. I miss Mutti, but it's not the same kind of miss. Everybody tries to cheer me up, but nothing works. Nothing changes. Think I'll give my red coat to Kat. It doesn't fit me anymore. Sleeves are too short. Hope Thanksgiving brings something to be grateful for.

Like an answer to a prayer, something did happen to be grateful for, sort of. A week before Thanksgiving Mutti wrote, saying she was much better and would be out of the San by spring. But the 'sort of' part had to do with what would happen when she did get out.

"Lizbeth," her letter read, "I have a wonderful opportunity to go to nursing school when I'm released from the

Sanatorium. Tante Anna and Onkel Chris, bless their hearts, have helped arrange it. It is one way, the only way, I can get to use my knowledge as a midwife. Best yet, they have also arranged for me to stay with a church family who live near the hospital where I'll be getting my training. There are two small bedrooms with a bath between and Lizbeth, my dearest daughter—this family, the Bergers, are more than willing to have you stay with me. Lizbeth, we get to be together again! I can't believe our good fortune. We are truly blessed. Of course I should tell you I'll be busy, I'll have to watch my health and you may be alone more often than I would like. But Mrs. Berger will be there a great deal of the time and you can be of help to her around the house. And you'll be going to a bigger, better school. Knowing you, you'll make friends easily. And we can also visit Central some weekends to see Tante Anna and Onkel Chris. I'm so excited I can hardly stand it. I love you so much and am so proud of you. Much, much love, Mutti."

Not long ago, I would have jumped right out of my skin for joy to be back with my beloved Mutti and away from this dreadful place, terrible food, noisy children, toilets without doors, strict rules—and the memory of those beatings the orphans got.

Some things had changed for the better, it was true. The toilets had curtains in front of them, and best of all, Tante Anna kept her promise that there would be no more beatings. After their visit to see the boys' backs, the trustees warned Father Gastmann that if such punishments were reported, he would be fired as superintendent. Father Gastmann resigned rather than give up his ideas of discipline. Onkel and Tante were put in charge and there were no more beatings. But without Georgie, there seemed to be no reason for staying here.

And yet, if I left to live with my mother, we would have to learn to know each other in a new way. I had changed, and my image of a widowed Mutti had changed, too.

I walked through some more grey days. There should have been some hope for the long future ahead of me. I should have dreamed my legs moved and I could run and get off the railroad tracks, but I could feel no hope and did not dream that I was free.

Then, the first winter snow came, gently falling, just like it was supposed to. I walked through the freshly fallen white flakes and it was like walking through a Christmas card. I climbed the stairs to the nursery and took off my blue coat. It was only Tante Anna and me now. Edna was working in town after school.

Tante Anna had her back to me and when she turned around, I saw her holding a new baby.

Tante's eyes crinkled at the corners just like they had that first day, but she wasn't smiling. She turned and lifted the corner of the baby's blanket for me to see. She didn't have to stoop down. I was now as tall as she.

What I saw took my breath away. It was a wrinkled up bit of baby, skinny fists, bluish skin, eyes tight shut.

"New born, Tante?" I asked.

Tante shook her head. "No, Lizbeth. A tiny baby girl, two or three months old, believe it or not. But neglected. She has the disease of neglect. She was found in a garbage can. She needs food, warm blankets. Most of all, she needs holding, rocking, loving. It will take a lot to make up for months of neglect. We have our hands full, Lizbeth."

We, she said. We. What a soft and wonderful word. How could I leave this place, I wondered with an ache all around my heart.

I sat down in the rocker and held out my arms to our new little orphan. Tante Anna placed her carefully on my lap and I held her close. I rocked her slowly and as I rocked, I leaned down and pressed my cheek against hers. Warmth flowed through me like liquid sunshine.

"Oh, Tante Anna," I whispered. "Can I name her? Could I call her Hope?"

"What a wonderful name," Tante answered, smiling broadly. "Of course. We'll have her baptized with that name. Hope. How about Hope Summers?" We both chuckled.

Not long ago, I had felt there was no hope about anything, anywhere. Now I was holding a baby that, in Tante's care, had a future before her.

I smiled at tiny Hope and she opened her eyes and gazed at me for a long moment. Then, she closed them again. I lifted the baby up to my shoulder, cradled her head against me, gently patting her back as I rocked. Tears welled up inside me and started to roll down my cheeks.

Images of my mother came to me. I imagined her holding me when I was a baby, patting me, loving me in just this way. She made some choices that were very painful for us both. But she never blamed anyone, and for years, bravely and at a cost to her health, did all she could to care for me. I'll never forget her words when she told me the truth about my father and herself. "Lizbeth, you'll never know how much I've loved you—every day of my life—and always will."

Now, she was alive and getting well, looking forward to being together again. I was not on orphan. I had a mother, a living, breathing, brave and wonderful mother who cared—a lot. How lucky I was. Blessed, Mutti had said in her letter.

Then, for the very first time, I thought I understood why Georgie had run away. She was not running away from Central—or from me. She was running toward her mother, as she said in her letter. More than anything in the world, more than her friendship with me or the safety of a warm bed, she wanted—and needed, to find her mother if she possibly could. Even though she had been abandoned, and maybe even because she had been, she needed to try and find her. And if she never found her, she might find someone who would be like a mother to her, with people who could become her family. She could laugh with them, dance with them, and be wild and wonderful with them.

Now, after all these days and weeks and months, the time had come. I could let Georgiana go.

It would be hard leaving Central, Tante Anna, the new baby. It would be hard going to another new school. But, more than anything in the whole, wide world I wanted to be with my very own mother, just like Georgiana did. I laid Baby Hope in her cradle, hugged Tante Anna, and left the nursery.

Now it was time I could start taking care of Mutti a little bit. *We* needed each other!

CHAPTER XX

MANY SEASONS HAVE come and gone since that long ago day when I stood with my mother on those cement steps that led up to the grey building we called the Big House. I clearly remember the fear that gripped me as I looked at the sign above the double door in black lettering. Central Orphans Asylum. I'd clung to my mother and begged her not to leave me there.

Yesterday, September 2, 1932, Mutti and I stood hand in hand looking up at the same building. That black sign was gone. The Big House no longer looked dark and forbidding but had been painted a soft, sunlight yellow.

After I left Central and went to live with Mutti in the city, we went back to visit many times. It had been good to see Kat and Leland and Clarence—and especially to watch Hope develop into a pretty, though shy, little girl. Every one delighted in her and the amazing progress she was making.

On each visit we saw some new change that had been made. The green lawn at the side of the Big House had transformed the entrance to Central Orphans Asylum and on the lawn, there was now a beautiful, low stone wall. On one of our visits Onkel Chris told us that some of the older boys helped him build it. In the flower bed above the wall, chrysanthemums—orange, lavender, white—were in full bloom. Tante Anna was so proud of that garden and the fact that the girls in the Brick House had helped her plant it.

The change we saw yesterday took my breath away. A huge sign in bronze lettering read: Central Children's Home. I can't explain the mixture of feelings that welled up inside of me as I looked at that sign. Children's *home*. Even the sound of it was beautiful.

I am not quite as much like Elizabeth of *Immensee*, that pale water lily, as I was when I lived here. I'm taller and stronger. I'm less afraid of making a mistake or doing the wrong thing. And yet, yesterday, a touch of sadness and a small tremble stirred inside me as I looked at that new sign. It reminded me of all of the changes in my life. In spite of my growing strength, I'm still afraid of changes, even if they're good ones. It's letting go of the known and stepping into the unknown, I guess. Coming here to Central, learning of Mutti's illness, meant letting my mother go, maybe for always. Leaving Central meant letting my wild orphan, Georgiana, fade into nearly forgotten memory.

Looking at that sign, Georgiana suddenly came alive in my mind. I wished with all my heart she could lend me her courage. I'll need it badly as I leave the safety of my life with Mutti and step into the unknown world that lies ahead of me. In a few more days I'll be leaving my mother again and going away to college. I am grateful for the opportunity, but still afraid.

Mutti's hand closed warmly over mine, pulling me back to the present. She looked at me and smiled. I smiled back and with a picture of Georgiana still in my mind, I squared my shoulders, walked up those steps with my mother and knocked on the big double door. After just a few moments, it opened. The two people I loved more than anyone other than Mutti stood there, big smiles on their faces and arms opened wide to greet us.

Compliments flowed back and forth among us—how wonderful and healthy Mutti looked, how tall and beautiful I had become. I was just beginning to believe it might be true, a little bit, anyway. Onkel Chris seemed finer and more dignified than ever, his hair completely silver, his handshake still strong and warm. And Tante, dearest Aunt Anna, had the same jolly laugh and glowing dark braid which even now did not have one grey hair.

Mutti answered their questions about her new job as charge nurse in the obstetric ward of Midtown Hospital. She glowed when she told them that at long last, she was able to use many of her skills as a midwife. Daily she felt appreciated by women in labor.

Then they all three turned to me. I opened my purse and took out the letter that promised to change the course of my life. I had received it on my eighteenth birthday in July. I handed it to Onkel Chris with trembling fingers.

Tante and Onkel read the letter together, smiles growing wide as they read that I had been accepted at Oakwood College, the school of my choice, in the Upper Midwest. The great surprise and joy was that I had been awarded a full scholarship, covering my tuition the first year.

"That is some birthday present," Tante Anna said as she took me in her arms.

Onkel Chris didn't say a word. He just reached for my hand with one of his, held the other out for my mother to take. Tante's warm hands completed the circle. She knew what Onkel wanted us to do. We bowed our heads and in his deep bass voice, he started us singing the blessing.

"Praise God from whom all blessings flow—"

When we finished the blessing, they took us to see more of the changes that had taken place at Central Children's Home.

On the way to the Brick House, Mutti and I exclaimed

over the vegetable and flower garden that had replaced the empty field.

"I had to have fresh vegetables for the children, something more than just cabbage," Tante said. "We have fresh greens and carrots and—and the best baking potatoes we could find to plant. No more fried potatoes here. Oh, once in a while, with scrambled eggs."

Onkel Chris laughed. "Anna knows what she wants, and we planned a way to get it. We find out what the children and teens are interested in and plan together, the children, young folks and us. They get to choose what jobs they like best. We work on rules together, too. They have a say in what consequences there should be for breaking a rule."

"No more bastards," Tante chimed in. "That word is forbidden. No matter where they came from, or how they got here, all are part of the family at Central. This is the children's, and young people's, *home*."

We walked along toward the Brick House, Mutti and Tante arm in arm, chatting away like old times. Onkel Chris walked along beside me and as we walked, I imagined walking beside my father just this way. I wondered if I would ever take up the search for him, my unknown, artist father. I had a long way to go before I would have the time and freedom to do so.

Thinking of my father, my feet began to drag. I did not want to enter the Brick House, especially not the dormitory. Sorrow for the losses of my life was too near the surface and close to my sadness, mixed with it, was my fear that I would not be brave enough to handle the pain of letting go the Known and facing the Unknown.

In my new found closeness to Onkel Chris, I found myself telling him how I felt. He put his arm around me, and said softly, "Lizbeth, I am proud of you." I could have wept for joy, imagining my father saying this to me.

I told him that part of me was afraid of leaving Mutti, afraid of going away to college, afraid I couldn't make it.

"Lizbeth, you've got the ability," he said. "Reach for the stars! Not many women do. There'll be help along the way—opportunities for work—more scholarships, maybe. But you must have determination. Most of all—you must be willing to risk!"

When he said that, Georgie's voice came to me, clear as the whippoorwill in the woods on that day the kids jumped in Jacob's Pool.

"Come on, Lizzie! Jump! I dare ya!"

Courage flowed into me like life-giving blood. I took Onkel's arm as we walked along in silence to the Brick House. The sitting room door was open, children's drawings on the walls, and—a piano!

The dormitory was empty because the children were out playing, or doing chores, but the cots had new covers, quilts with lively colors on each one. I sat down on the cot that had been mine and looked over at the one where Georgiana had lain. I put my hand on the pillow that held her black, messy curls.

A gentle sadness washed over me. I felt again all the hurt I had felt when I looked at the empty cot beside mine. I could hear our voices, complaining, giggling, dreaming our way through the years of our change from childhood to near-grown-upness. I said a prayer for Georgie and left the room.

After we said "good-bye" to Tante and Onkel, with warm hugs and promises to keep in touch, we left Central Children's Home, walked to the train station, and traveled home.

When Mutti and I got home I went into my room to be alone. I wanted to remember all that I had experienced and learned that day and write it all down. I got out my diary and began to read. I stopped when I found this entry:

November 15, 1928: Oh, Georgiana, where are you? Why didn't you talk it over with me before you left?

'Tis not knowing where you've gone
that leaves me so alone.
I've tried to let you go
But oh, it hurts me so.
I need your rage, I need your dare
I need your wild, unruly hair.

Not even Tante Anna's comfort helps me. Not even knowing Mutti is getting well.

The leaves have started to turn again. Soon, they will come fluttering down, sounding like baby rattles. In the safety of my room in my own home, with my own much loved mother, I think about the gypsies. I wondered if this year they will wander down the street so near Central Children's Home, their wagon wheels squeaking, pots and pans clanging and banging, straggly, dirty, free. Will townsfolk still lock their doors and watch the wild gypsies through curtained windows, suspicious, fascinated and afraid of these amazing people they know nothing about.

I asked Onkel about the gypsies on one of our visits and he said he still questions the gypsies who come through in the spring and fall. No one had seen or heard of Putja's band in all this time. No one knew of any Putja, didn't understand,—or wouldn't tell him. No Putja, no La Lubja—no Georgiana.

In just a few more days, I'll be going away to college, and then, if I work hard and keep up my courage, maybe even medical school. I will try my hardest to become a doctor someday, as my mother wanted so much to be. A doctor who writes poetry on the side.

Years of hard work lie ahead of me. When I become a doctor, I'd like to do something to keep orphans, or any children for that matter, from getting beaten so badly. Something to help midwives be allowed to deliver babies. Something, in some way, for the gypsies. And maybe, just maybe, I might find some trace of Georgiana. How wonderful it would be to know she is well and happy.

In the meantime, I am grateful for all I learned those years at Central. I learned how to get along with different kinds of people. I learned during those years what a truly wonderful person my mother was; but that if I had to, I could get along without her always nearby.

Most important of all, I learned, in the deepest part of me, that I never really lost Georgiana, my wild orphan, my first best friend. She is a part of who I now am—more courageous, more daring than I ever imagined I could be. And if I never see her again, I'll always be deeply grateful that for a short time, she was a part of my life.

ACKNOWLEDGMENTS

WILD ORPHAN is dedicated to all those children everywhere who have experienced the loneliness, the fear, and feelings of abandonment that are a part of starting life without knowing where one came from, or who one's parents were. I have known some of these children, and I am grateful to them for deepening my understanding and appreciation of their pain. Their courage has been an inspiration to me, and a powerful incentive for the writing of this book.

I am grateful, too, for the time and patience several children, not orphans, have given to reading the manuscript and sharing their honest opinions as to how "good a read" this story was for them and offering some valuable suggestions. Thank you, Cally Rice and Karin Tia Fouchi of Mankato, Minnesota.

My gratitude also includes Louisa Smith, retired professor of Children's Literature at Minnesota State University at Mankato, Minnesota, and Cindy Lundeen, media specialist for Elementary Education in Iowa, whose careful reading and critiquing of the manuscript was most helpful.

Ellen Hawley, editor, Daniel Hoisington, publisher, my husband, Fred Doty and daughter Kristan . . . thank you for your insightful and unwavering support.

And thank you, Grace Lee, my loyal friend and supporter for many years as we journeyed together "On The Way To Over The Hill." Without your encouragement, love, and shared experience as a published writer, I probably would not have stuck to the task. You were and are a "Guide To Living Gracefully!"

ABOUT THE AUTHOR

KATHRYN ADAMS DOTY was born in New Ulm in 1920, the daughter of Christian Hohn—pastor of the German Methodist Church—and his wife Anna. At age six Kathryn moved with her parents to Warrenton, Missouri, when her father took the post of executive secretary of the Central Wesleyan Orphan Home. During teenage years she lived in Crookston, Minnesota, where her father pastored the local Methodist Church. She enrolled at Hamline University in Saint Paul in 1937.

Two years later, the Lux Radio Show hosted a Gateway to Hollywood contest with the winners receiving a contract from RKO Studios. Encouraged to enter by her drama teacher, she won the Midwest tryouts. Although she lost in the national finals, director Gregory La Cava called and gave her a role in *Fifth Avenue Girl* with Ginger Rogers. Over the next few years, under the stage name of Kathryn Adams, she had roles in dozens of movies under the old studio system. Other films include *The Hunchback of Notre Dame*, *If I Had My Way* (with Bing Crosby), *The Invisible Woman* (with John Barrymore), and Alfred Hitchcock's *Saboteur*.

Her major roles, though, were in so-called "B" movies. She played the leading lady opposite fellow Minnesotan Richard Arlen in *Black Diamonds* and Donald Woods in *Love, Honor and Oh Baby*. She starred with cowboy hero Johnny Mack Brown in three Westerns and had featured roles in the serial cliff-hangers *Sky Raiders* and *Junior G-Men of the Air*.

In 1941, she married fellow actor Hugh Beaumont—best-known as the father in the television series *Leave It To*

Beaver. Universal Studios wanted them to conduct the actual wedding on the set of Irene Dunne's *Unfinished Business* as a publicity stunt, but Kathryn refused. Later, the married couple teamed up in the 1946 Michael Shane detective movie, *Blonde for a Day*. After that, she retired from the silver screen to raise a family.

Later, she earned a Master's Degree in Educational Psychology and embarked on a distinguished career as a psychologist. After retirement, she returned to her first love—writing. She moved back to Minnesota in 1977, where she lives with her husband, Fred Doty.

In 2004 Edinborough Press published her novel, *A Long Year of Silence*. Set in New Ulm, Minnesota, it tells the story of Emma Altenberg, whose world is turned upside down when the United States enters World War I. Anti-German hysteria sweeps through Minnesota, disrupting the lives of friends and family. A sixteen-year-old minister's daughter, Emma struggles with the challenge of relationships with her parents and her peers. The novel won the Midwest Book Award, given by the Midwest Independent Publishers Association, and was a finalist for the Minnesota Book Award in young adult fiction.